LILA'S MIND:

MONSTERS, GODS, DEMONS, FAIRIES, AND WITCHES

Text and photos from the film

A monster called Lila

with Eva Henger

and Giampaolo Innocentini

by ENRICO BERNARD

© entertainmentart@gmx.net

The sentimental-emotional world of Lila

One of the fundamental premises of psychoanalysis consists in the belief that what is formed in the first period of human life, regarding the emotional-sentimental world, remains in the subconscious mind of the adult person. From this point of view, one can understand how the *internal objects* of Lila are characterized by a very primitive mental structure due to the absence of internalized parental figures.

The lack of this internalization is not due to the physical death of the parents, occurred by a car accident (or escape from gas), although contributing to the deterioration of Lila's inner psyche situation. Something happened before, from the first moments of her life. *The lack of the process of internalization* that alone can avoid an idealization or demonization of the absence of parental figures.

The sentimental-emotional mental structure of Lila, the protagonist of the film, can be understood only internally by her primitive dimension. One is dealing with a little girl as she is portrayed in different sequences, not only as she appears, child-like in an explicit way, at the end of the film. We are facing a symbiotic mind, that is still strongly connected to the mother, in a state of great confusion, capable of only getting excited, but not enjoying, let alone suffering. Fantasies, desires, anguishes, anxieties, and fears dominate her mind. Incapable of *an inner psyche and inner personal* relationship, of a calm communication between the various parts of the "Self" and with the other persons, without falling into persecutory and depressive forms. Her mental mechanisms of division, of projective identification, and introspection are "massive", that is, very intense, uncontrollable from a very primitive mind such as Lila's. A mind capable only of generating *monsters, gods, or demons* and at the same time, impotent and unable to dominate them, lacking a paternal figure, a *container,* for all these intense disturbing sufferings.

We save in our inner world, even as adults, parental figures that can be defined as *gods* or *demons,* who dominate in distorting *our representation of the world and of ourselves* and projecting out of us heroes, divinities, fairies, witches and also *monsters.* Literature, poetry, and art, in all their forms, have been the first expression, a long time before film and psychoanalysis.

Therefore, not creating wonderment or astonishment, the fact that the human mind in general, *may create monsters.* But most of all Lila's anguishes, anxieties, and fears become more understandable, immersed in a desperate solitude, she can only defend herself, projecting outside of herself these internalized monsters: "No Sirs, the Bad, The Monster, it's us!", is exclaimed powerfully at the beginning of the film. With extraordinary beauty and capability, representative of Lila's inner psyche world is the sequence in which the different figures of nude men and of women move slowly and direct themselves towards her shoulders. Depictions of parts of Herself persecuted and terrorized, fostered by the anguish of solitude in which Lila finds herself.

Lila sings: The treasure chest of thoughts/ mine which are black/ knows every torment/ which distresses inside/ I remain alone and I am afraid / of my dark zone!". And she adds: "My parents are dead, I have no friends nor parents. Left alone." Be it the psychology of the developmental age that psychoanalysis underlines the fact that above all childhood is the age characterized by this aspect. It can be present, in an accentuated way by the pathological modalities observed, even in other phases, as that of latency, pre-adolescence, but also in maturity and old age.

Lila's inner optical.

This projective mental activity of inner monsters is defensive in that it gives the impression of liberating the inner world from these internal objects which unfold in addition to the function of mediators from the external world. They are the inner optical through which Lila sees the world. Therefore, she is afraid and worried from the presence of all these monsters that attack her shoulders.

But the internal objects can be persecutors and can strike and cut like a knife that wounds and makes Lila bleed. Symbolically amazingly effective, is the sequence in which a bloody knife traverses the nude body of the girl.

It is noted that in the phase or primitive position, the external tormenting objects, originated by suffering by the absence of the good object, are characterized by feelings of hate, anger, and resentment that are projected onto the external objects.

It is in this phase that are implemented the primitive, mental subconscious processes of splitting and of projective identification, of denial, of idealization and of demonization, in massive form, to defend herself from mental psychic suffering. An excess or defect of these modalities can produce an altered perception of external reality, which (reality), connected to an altered perception of the inner reality, can determine neurotic or psychotic suffering and, in extreme cases, irrational and blinding forms.

What an ugly dream!

The film can be read as a dream, rich with symbols and a sentimental story, very intense and complex. Through her own dreams Lila puts on a performance connotated by her feelings. Seeing how every person, from the psyche point of view is her own subconscious depiction of the internal world which she identifies with and through which she knows the exterior world, it is of extreme importance the existence of a *rational internal depiction and not distorted* by her own inner world for having also a depiction more fitting of the external world.

But such an inner rational depiction implies the ability of the human individual to accept reality regardless of whether it would be pleasing or not. This is the difficulty of Lila. The reality is bitter, it is full of pain and suffering. It is difficult also to know enjoyment because it implies knowing suffering. In Lila's dreams, as in every dream, she attempts in a union of the most significant elements in the inner world have a religious and sacred meaning, referring to the internalized parental figures. The sequences are multiple in the film through which it is possible to identify to this emotional story, full of suffering and ambiguity, narrated through a process of divisions, of projective identification, of denial. For example, it is significant, the symbolic gesture with which Lila carries the two lit candles on her chest. The ambiguity of the candle scene can be taken as the gesture of wax poured on the chest. She cannot not burn like every desire not satisfied can "hurt", one could remain indeed "burnt".

Also the symbolic gesture of eating spaghetti on the torso of the girl can be read as the projection of an intense and irrepressible desire of Lila. So strong is the desire of a relationship is to "blend and to mistake herself with the loved person (I would eat you!)." But this is not possible, therefore it is better to move this desire to the spaghetti allowing to devour it. This is so difficult for Lila, the little girl to hold onto a desire! It is better to consider it to be a dangerous desire and how it should be flushed down the toilet. Perhaps it is not what we do with every "natural need"? It is dealing with getting rid of "poop or piss". From here the devaluation and the denial of every desire and every need because these are the causes of suffering if they do not get satisfied. Here is why Lila does not allow herself to fall in love, to love, to get involved emotionally and sentimentally. "She is beautiful, but without a soul." She has a beautiful body to show, a body that can solicit the voyeuristic component of the male, but not up to the task of seducing, if not as a little girl whether desperate and alone, she is not able as far as asking to be restrained and protected.

LILA AND HER MONSTER IN THE MIRROR

Who is the monster? Where does he hide in ourselves? In our dreams? Our desires? Our fears? An erotic surreali thriller: a dangerous gam of evoking nightmares.

The setting of the story is an empty restaurant room in a wooded aerea of a Nordic region bordering the Swiss Alps. The play begins as it is still dark, early in the morning. Empty tables await the arrival of patrons. A beautiful and provocative waitress moves nervously around the room. Suddenly a stranger arrives, dressed in black, claiming that his car has broken down. In a matter of minutes begins a dramatic duet between the stranger (the monster? the devil?) and the beautiful girl (a victim) as they begin to battle with a series of questions and accusations. The shole dialogue is about bringing to the surface not so much her memories but Lila's hidden feelings, fears, anxieties, animalistic instinct, sexuality, and intimate fantasies. The restaurant room soon becomes a psychoanalytical and oneiric playground. In the final scene, just as the first rays of sunlight come into the room, the mystery surrounding is resolved. Is daylight cenceling a bad dream? And, is this the beginning of a new day and perhaps the start of a new life for Lila?

A Monster called Lila.

When Bernard first staged *Un mostro di nome Lila* (1995) he would have never guessed that his new play would soon become one of his most talked about work. Eros and Thanatos, the erotic and the nightmarish, Faust and Freud, are all perfectly fused in this extremely intense drama that Italian, Swiss and German reviewers defined as a most fascinating "erotic psychological thriller". In this one act play Bernard leaves behind his familiar socio-political criticism in order to focus primarily on the private and hidden sphere of the human psyche. It is indeed a play that allows the author to play freely with Freudian symbols and double meanings. The setting for the story is an empty restaurant room in a wooded area of a Nordic region bordering the Swiss Alps. The characters are a girl and a mano The play begins as it is still dark, early in the morning. Empty tables await the arrivai of patrons. A beautiful and provocative waitress moves nervously around the room. Suddenly a stranger arrives, dressed in black, claiming that his car has broken down. In a matter of minutes begins a dramatic duet between the stranger (the monster? the devil?) and the beautiful girl (a victim?) as they begin to battle with a series of questions and accusations. The whole dialogue is about bringing to the surface not so much her memories but Lila's hidden feelings, fears, anxieties, animalistic instinct, sexuality, and intimate fantasies. The restaurant room soon becomes a psychoanalytical and oneiric playground. The dialogues, as well as the familiar symbols such as a stranger dressed in black, and a beautiful young woman alone in an isolated house in the woods, provide the material and images for a suspenseful erotic mystery. In the verbal exchanges, at times accompanied by brief erotic physical contacts between Lila and the stranger, the audience witnesses how the invented images of a bad dream, or better, of a nightmare, becomes a cruel reality. During the entire heated argument Lila, although fighting back and at times blaming the stranger for her troubles, ends up making confession of her deep feelings of guilt and of her past sexual sins. In the final scene, just as the first rays of sunlight come into the room, the mystery surrounding Lila is resolved. Is daylight canceling a bad dream? And, is this the beginning of a new day and perhaps the start of a new life for Lila? Once the battle between the monster and the victim is over it becomes clear that the duel was a manifestation of the struggle between Lila's (her "dark zone") subconscious and her superficial social facade put on for herself and for others. In fact, from the dialogues we learn that Lila has grown up seeking in and through her sexuality the warmth of human affection. However, her alter ego has decided to rebel. Doctor Jekyll and Mr. Hyde, light and darkness, love and sex, Eros and Thanatos, have all resorted to battle one another. But which side of Lila has won? *A Monster Called Lila* is unquestionably Enrico Bernard's most powerful play that focuses specifically on emotions and psychological issues related to guilt. It is also the play that has won the most approval from audiences and critics wherever it has been staged in Italy, France and Switzerland. By the same token with *A Monster Called Lila* some critics began to speak of Bernard's new interests in treating light eroticism on stage.

A MONSTER CALLED LILA

by Enrico Bernard

© entertainmentart@gmx.net

Characters:

Lila
A Stranger

INCIPIT

Is nature good or evil? The snowy peaks are a stunning backdrop: from up there one looks down on the earth and the soul of the observer feels as though it could range over infinite space, up towards and beyond the vault of the sky. But, beware! Beneath the snow covered summit await deep gullies and terrifying crevasses, untamed torrents whose fury pummels the tops of trees like a menacing murmur of death. Then, all at once, the water vanishes, as though swallowed up by the earth, as though sucked into its very bowels. It gets lost among dark, infernal meanderings, in the caverns in which spectral formations appear and disappear in the beams of the flashlights of speleologists who descend into the underground abyss covered by nature's strange messages: stalagmites and stalactites that, like a horrid mouth, rip through the anguished silence with the sound of the eternal dripping that beats out time's timelessness in the void.

Nature, then, can be neither good nor evil; neither absolutely beautiful nor ugly, precisely because without the gullies and the precipices, no peak could jut out majestically into the infinite. And without the crystal clear water rushing through the mysterious mazes of caves and caverns, there would be no water to spurt up limpid and pure to course once more down the valley and reflect the azure of the sky. Nothing in nature is good or bad given that the instinctual forces which lead a wild animal to kill are necessary for the survival of the species, for harmony, for equilibrium. Human nature would be subject to this kind of call of the wild, were it not for culture which tames the instincts, isolating them in our being and then projecting their bestial essence outside ourselves, into another, one of us who is Evil, into something different and alien which we call MONSTROUS but which we might perhaps more fittingly call

Those of you about to sit through this performance should harbour no illusions of coming away from it consoled and cheered: abandon all hope you who enter here! A sudden scream will surprise, unnerve, terrify you. And you'll ask yourselves: can it be me who is screaming, or, instead, is somebody out there mad at me? No, the truth is, that to descend into hell, all you have to do is look within. We are, all of us to a man, failed monsters. So if you really want to defeat Evil, it's time to start fighting it where it resides: inside ourselves. Nor is it conceivable that the monstrosity which unsettles and terrifies us is the handiwork of an unusual, foreign creature that is monstrous! Something born out of nothingness that will be sucked back into the void after a miserable existence on earth on the margin of so-called normality. No, ladies and gentlemen, Evil, the Monster, why it's us! And rooting it out is not easy, since we would need the courage of performing surgery on ourselves. We are born with instincts, with the taste of blood in our mouths, with the cutting of the umbilical cord (and being born is more painful than dying). This unleashes the daemon of life which takes control of us and with a great deal of difficulty, through the evolution of conscience, through education, through culture, one manages (not always, not entirely) to uproot it. But the road is filled with snares and hurdles nontheless. The journey is through darkness and uphill. Those who lose the way leading to the centre of their being, to the knowledge of our resident "friend" the monster, really risk ending up like the heroine of the play about to begin.

SCENE:

The inside of a mountain lodge on the border between the Italian and German-speaking area in the Alps: it might be present-day southern Tyrol or Canton Ticino. It's 5 a.m. on a bitter winter morning. It's still night and in the semidarkness can be heard the wind and the rustling of the forest whose shadows on the window in the backdrop seem to be crazed spirits unable to rise towards heaven. The howling of a lone wolf. A sound begins to thump in the silence and grows louder and louder. A heart, Lila's heart, is beating furiously. A scream.

Lila enters. She is already dressed but still has to comb her hair and pull up her stockings. She will do this with gestures suggestive of subtle forms of autoeroticism.

LILA: What a night! I couldn't shut my eyes. The wind felt like it was going right through the walls. And I was huddling in a corner of the bed, wrapped in blankets, my head hiding under the pillow. I trembled as I heard strange voices which made my skin crawl: infernal whistling which emanated from visions of ... of ... (it's hard to say it, the very thought makes my skin crawl!) of dismembered corpses, horribly piled up in my addled brain which just couldn't get to sleep. (She sings softly, combing her hair.)

The spectre of my imagining
how black and ever darkening,
it knows each pain and sorrow
stirring within my marrow:
I am left feeling all alone
so terrified of my dark zone.

A nightmare, who can say why!... It was me, as though I were two people, approaching the bed in which I myself was lying defenceless, both victim and murderer at once. And the blade of the knife which I simultaneously wielded and thrust into myself, gave off sinister flashes of light... And what words I heard coming from my mouth: unrepeatable! But it wasn't me talking; it was another me whom I didn't know and who...(she hides her face in her hands) Ah! Good thing the night is over, or almost! In the summer, at this time, one would hear birds...! Instead it must be the darkness forming the chrysalis of day which is thus born already extinguished ... (surprised by her own words). How can I be saying such things, I'm a simple, shy, small town girl ... And yet, at least while the night lasts, I talk like a poet spurred on by his daemon ... Daemon? So then it's the devil in me that is speaking: like a thin voice which whispers the lines to those who then deliver them, that's what the wind is! It is the Devil that makes the trunks snap and the dried, frozen branches of the oaks rustle until the trees sound out the names, the things, the thoughts which someone plants in me like sperm ... What did I say? My God, what did I say? ... (She makes the sign of the cross) My mind is wandering in the darkness like some blind man in the light of day. The unreal quality created by the penumbra in which real things vanish to take on new shapes is frightening. So the shadow of the back of a chair is transformed into the satanic leer of the table, and the chandelier that swings back and forth in a draft of air is nothing but the bat into which He morphs, the Lord of Darkness whom we bear within us, the darkness which He illuminates with his spectral light: and that, precisely, is his name, Lucifer, he who bears light, but what a light!

The swan of my imagining
how black and ever darkening
it knows each pain and sorrow

stirring within my marrow:
and I am left here all alone
so terrified of my dark zone

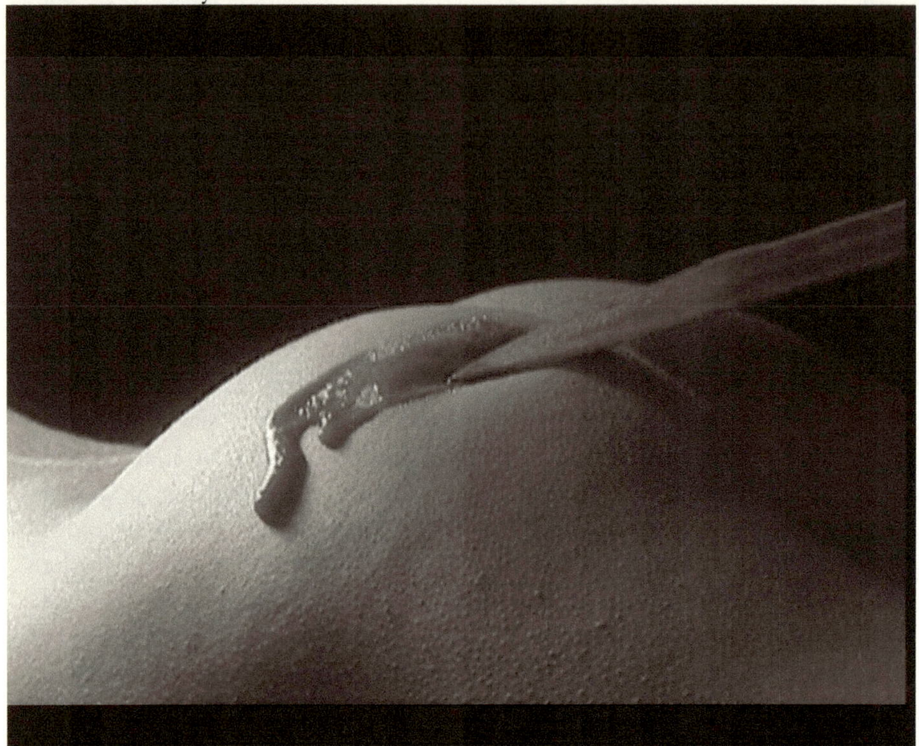

Shush, Lila, shush. After all it's not your fault if summer's not here yet
and if the day hasn't yet broken through with its tumid phallus... Why am
I saying "phallus"? What am I saying? I'm using Satan's words, maybe ...
Shush, be silent, mouth! Don't say things you don't know, which you
can't know about. And if I tell you that you can't know them, you have to
believe me! (Pauses) Good girl, Lila, good girl. Now stay calm and think
that soon the window will be bathed in light, the light will fill the room
and penetrate your eyes and into your brain and impregnate it ... Light?
His light, maybe, wants to penetrate and impregnate me, Lucifer's light!
And I won't be able to say "Get thee behind me!" since I've possessed
myself, opening myself to him, the swine, the pig, and I've soiled myself
with his excrement, with his urine, with the fetid saliva he left on my
nipples, on my lips ... everywhere, like a reminder, an infernal warning
that says: you are flesh! But the flesh, Lila, withers away, and the Father
knows that you have sinned: he has seen, he has heard ... Enough, Lila,
it's enough now. You've talked far too much with his voice, too many evil
words have passed your lips. And then, the dreams are so unreal that it
isn't even worthwhile believing them! Are they of any use to anyone? Well,

maybe to ourselves, to hurt us, or for the evil we have within us which has to find an escape hatch somewhere... but what do I know about dreams! Why am I here agonizing when there is still so much to do to prepare the place before opening time ... (as if pulled back by the thread out of which she was weaving her monologue) Dreams are only places of uncertainty in which reason is an empty shell, like the skull of a dead man ... Ah! What thoughts I keep having! Stop, you silly little head, before it's too late... The croissants haven't come yet. I'll have to heat up yesterday's; nobody will notice anyway, what with their mouths still full of sleep ... I had a really strange dream which I can't figure out; it was as if things had no substance to them and I was floating around them. They offered no resistance to my body which wasn't there at all, but I was falling into them as though there was nothing to them. The very blankets seemed to be waves washing over me, stifling my breath, my reality in the void: an immense ocean of the mind was buffeting within me dragging me along towards a bottomless pit. And, at the end of that abyss, the beast rolled its fiery eyes ... Oh, it's horrible! (She covers her face with her hands)

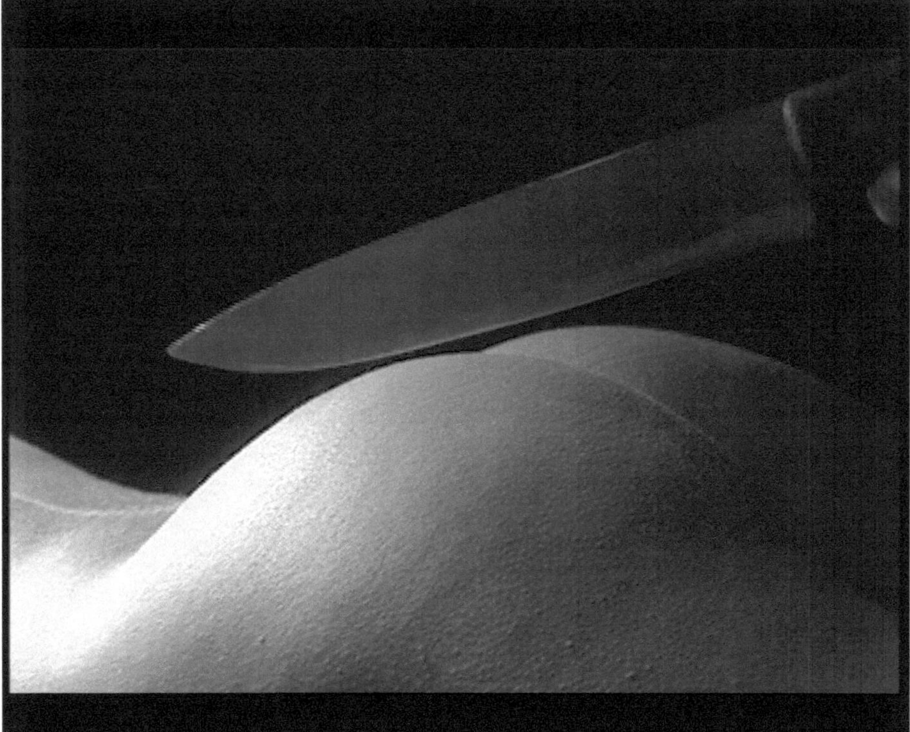

Behind Lila, who is unaware of his presence, appears the Stranger. Limping slightly, he wears a nondescript overcoat and a wide-brimmed, black hat and is carrying a suitcase.

STRANGER: Such ugly dreams, Miss, are better left alone.
LILA: (Surprised) Who...are you?
STRANGER: I'd just like to have some breakfast, if that's possible.
LILA: I didn't hear you come in.
STRANGER: Yes, I know. I was quiet on purpose. I didn't want to disturb your...what shall I call it? ... Ah, yes, your soliloquy.
LILA: You might just as well call it blathering.
STRANGER: Don't be too harsh. Perhaps we might say it was a harmless interior monologue. Anyway, don't worry: it's really nothing to worry about and certainly in not compromising. Believe me. At most a state of momentary mental alteration due to, oh, I don't know, the full moon or being overly stimulated by the warmth of the blankets which sometimes causes the mind to turn the body into an ill-defined entity dominated by the PP, that is, the Pleasure Principle, the primordial instinct of human beings. What you in German call, if I'm not mistaken, Lustprizip.
LILA: I wouldn't know, but ... am I dreaming? (Tentatively) You are here, aren't you? I mean, you're real ... Or should I pinch myself...? A second ago you seemed to be transparent, as though the light went through you, a strange sort of light, a light unlike anything found on the face of the earth.
STRANGER: Transparent, me? Perhaps: I haven't eaten anything since last night and I still haven't had breakfast.
LILA: But, excuse me for insisting, you seem to be really made of air ... as though you'd been created out of the wind whistling through the chinks in the window, in the spaces between the boards ... Are you sure you're not a...?
STRANGER: Oh, that's rich! You think I'm a ghost? No, sorry to disappoint you. I'm not part of your dream or, if you prefer, your nightmare (even though you do seem quite capable of dreaming with your eyes open). In short, I'm not that "beast" which, I don't know how, you managed to see as you looked out over the precipice into the abyss ... Am I right? No, no. Look, let me tell you one last time. I'm just a customer. Maybe your first, at this hour, but you have to start with someone. So it's either me or someone else. Or are you still closed?
LILA: We're about to open.
STRANGER: That's not a very convincing answer. Don't sit on the fence: are you open or closed? Say it loud and clear. Otherwise, I'm leaving.
LILA: In a hurry, are we?

STRANGER: Unfortunately, I'll have to be going soon. Besides, I think I took a wrong turn and I'm somewhat lost. When I noticed that the paved road ended and the forest began I said to myself: bloody hell, you're about to end up like that master poet, Dante ... right into the dark wood, you see? I kept going around in circles and then I saw that the sign of this place was lit. So I stopped the car and said to myself, this looks like a place frequented by hunters, so they'll probably be opening soon, I

said to myself, and so I got out...

LILA: And what did you say to yourself once you were out ...

STRANGER: I get it, you're making fun of me. Quite right, I did get lost like a ninny ... I got off the highway because that straight road was driving me crazy ... you see, I've been driving all night. So I got off and took the state highway, just so the odd curve would force me to stay awake, then I got onto the provincial one-lane with curves everywhere, until I finally ended up on this sort of mule track ...

LILA: You're lucky. They just paved it. They wanted to tear down the forest to break through to the other side and connect it with the main highway. But then the environmentalists came in and the plan was put on hold. Too bad, it would have been good for business.

STRANGER: Great, so instead of a lodge in the middle of a forest, I would have found a gas station with self-serve pumps open twenty-four seven.

LILA: It's a diner.

STRANGER: For truck drivers.

LILA: Better that than hunters with their guns. They give me the jitters.

STRANGER: That doesn't sound good. It means you haven't completely divested yourself of your Electra complex or, as Sigmund says, you're still suffering from penis envy.

LILA: I don't understand. I don't know who this Sigmund is. I find it stupid to talk like that. It's disrespectful to talk like that to me, if I may say so. You're taking such liberties because you know I'm too embarrassed to reply in kind. So, please be nice; stop assailing me with your double meanings. I know where you're headed with all that stuff, anyway.

STRANGER: Look, quite frankly, your sexual frustrations don't really have anything to do with me. All I want is a cup of coffee and for you to tell me how to find my way out of this ... well, oh what the heck, let's call it by its real name, out of this dark wood, there, I've said it.

LILA: You'll have to wait a few minutes for the coffee, the pressure hasn't built up yet.

STRANGER: I'll wait!

LILA: Why don't you sit down?

STRANGER: Are you kidding? I've been sitting all night driving! I'd like to stretch my legs a bit, otherwise how will I manage the next thousand kilometres.

LILA: And where are you headed?

STRANGER: I don't know. All the world's a stage after all.

LILA: Are you headed south?

STRANGER: Yes, I'm going to hell, if you don't mind.

LILA: Don't get angry. We have different customs here. The town is small, we all know each other, there are no secrets ... Besides, you can go wherever you wish, even to the south. There are fine people there, too. Just like you and me. Am I forgiven?

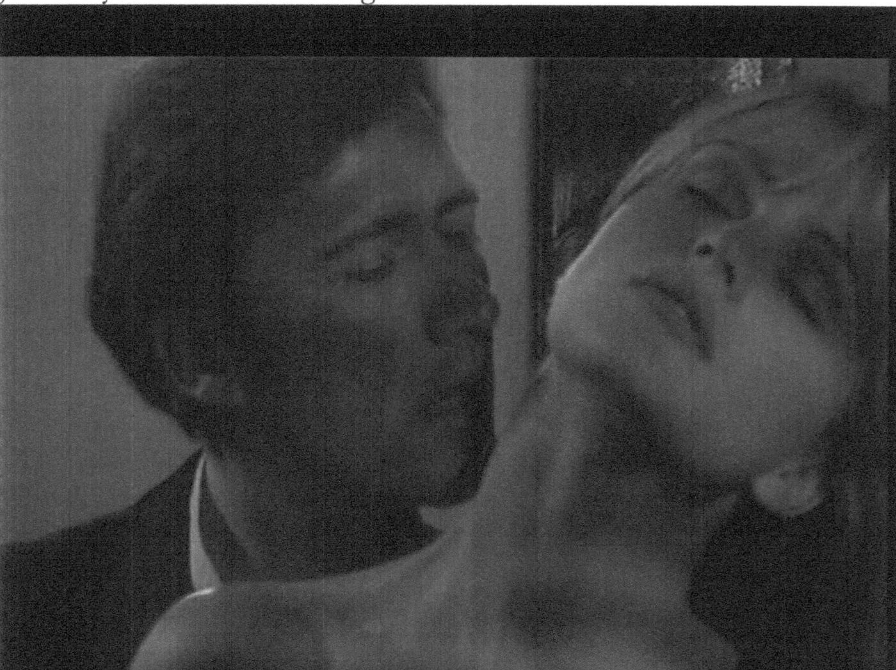

STRANGER: No, no. It's you who must forgive me. I'm saying such things because I'm tired, I assure you. I'm not my usual self. On the contrary...

LILA: It's I who can't seem to mind my own ... And then this stuff about south and north, well, it's time to put an end to it, as if there weren't also east and west. (Changes tone) You know, I've had a very disturbing night ... Hey, is it still night?

STRANGER: Neither night nor day, a vague region between the two in which the creatures of darkness - the ones that inhabit our dreams - dart quickly back to where they came from, before the sun's radiance has pushed back the darkness.

LILA: You say such difficult things to figure out ... and yet I seem to understand, or I think I understand ... strange!

STRANGER: And that surprises you?

LILA: Shouldn't it?

STRANGER: They say this is the time of day for suffering souls ...

LILA: Like mine!

STRANGER: Those that haven't gone to hell but which haven't managed to make it to heaven. It's a purgatory in which monsters flit about that have never had the courage to fully realize themselves in their complete, total bestiality: unfinished monsters, roughly sketched in, bits and pieces of monsters that don't make any sense, born out of, at most, a paltry imaginations, fatuous flames of our thoughts which fire up to keep themselves warm in their dramatic abstraction, in their tragic cerebral isolation and which are somewhat, if I may say it, wanker-like! A mind jerking off on the thought that it is creating light, like a light bulb proud of its glare with the sun shining bright in the sky, So, what's the point of floating one's monstrous thoughts in this purgatory in which everything is just smoke and mirrors, form without substance?

LILA: I'm sorry, but I just don't think I can follow you.

STRANGER: I was saying: why, why just think in abstract terms about

the monster lurking within us instead of ... Am I right?
LILA: I don't know, and I don't want to know.
STRANGER: Or are you afraid of saying it?
LILA: What if I were?
STRANGER: What can it possibly be? Out with it!
LILA: Fears, only vague fears, which, as you aptly point out, are abstract.
STRANGER: (Reassuring) You'll see that with the first light of dawn these ancestral (and somewhat puerile, I'm sorry to say) fears will vanish; and in the transparent chalice of life (sorry to keep harping, but you've got to, you've got to!) blood will no longer flow; no, it will be a green lymph, a vital fluid, like in the leaves and buds of springtime. Happy?
LILA: Get away from me; shoo! Can't you see I'm working?
STRANGER: You're committing the rather gross error of putting your blind trust in the day that's about to break but which is still not upon us, if you will allow me. A sun which hasn't risen yet is a bit like interest at the bank which hasn't yet matured.

LILA: You're pretty good with words, you are.
STRANGER: It's the truth. Daylight favours lucid, rational thought, while darkness unleashes in the mind ... But, maybe it's better to let well enough alone. You're right. Too embarrassing . (Pause) You have nice legs, you know?

LILA: I do? They're crooked.

STRANGER: The legs of an amazon. Do you ride?

LILA: Yes, but not a horse, a motorcycle.

STRANGER: Ah, the sporty type then.

LILA: When I have bad thoughts, I slip on my helmet and take off. I have no idea where I'll end up, I just ride and ride, maybe even in circles, like an idiot. It would not be the first time...

STRANGER: What kinds of thoughts? Sexual, yes?

LILA: I beg your pardon!

STRANGER: You're quite at liberty not to talk about them, mercy yes!

LILA: I don't believe this!

STRANGER: I, on the other hand, if I were you, would talk about them.

LILA: And why would I do that?

STRANGER: Too much pressure, the machine might explode.

LILA: And what makes you think that it's under pressure?

STRANGER: It's obvious.

LILA: Really? And how can you say that?

STRANGER: From the steam. You can't see that the espresso machine's about to go boom because you've got your back to it, but I can. Hurry, before it blows up! Jesus, I told you it's about to explode! Do something! (From behind the counter a dense vapour is pouring out)

LILA: Yes, Yes ... (angry, to the machine, working its knobs) Du, Hexe!

STRANGER: Motors and females, what joys what travails!

LILA: Don't be petty.

STRANGER: I'm only trying to kill time. I'm hungry as a wolf, and if I don't get a coffee immediately, I'm going to start howling. You want to hear me? Here goes, howwwwwl!

LILA: Well, you'll just have to wait, Mr. Were Wolf. (To herself) He looks like one!

STRANGER: Well, I don't want to brag...

LILA I've emptied the machine because the valve gets blocked sometimes and it won't flush. The steam will have to build up again... You'll have to be patient.

STRANGER: From a customer to a patient, then. Some service! Do I get a tip!

LILA: Meanwhile I'll set the tables for breakfast. Why don't you give me a hand instead of being in the way?

STRANGER: Oh, no. There's no way that's going to happen!.

LILA: Lazy bones.

STRANGER: Why should I help you set up?

LILA: So I'll save time.

STRANGER: And what do I get out of it if I help?

LILA: Your coffee. Did you want something else? A croissant?

STRANGER: Whatever your heart desires.

LILA: Fine! I'll give you a croissant, as soon as they get here from the bakery.

STRANGER: And if they don't come?

LILA: Why shouldn't they come?

STRANGER: Because of the psychosis ... the monster's psychosis.

LILA: What monster? What are you talking about?

STRANGER: Don't pretend you don't know. I wasn't born yesterday.

LILA: You're just passing through. What do you know about what's going on in this town?

STRANGER: I read the papers. The thing's made the national news. And ... you, don't you read them?

LILA: Yes, yes ... When I have time.

STRANGER: And ... Don't you listen to the radio?

LILA: When I have time.

STRANGER: And ... don't you watch television?

LILA: (Annoyed) When I have time.

STRANGER: And when will you have time?

LILA: When you leave me alone so I can set up, seeing as you refuse to help me.

STRANGER: Well, if it makes you happy ...

LILA: I bet it's the first time you do housework.

STRANGER: The first and last.

LILA: And what does your wife say about that?

(She hands him a tray with dishes on it)

STANGER: I'm not married.

LILA: Well you have a girlfriend, a fiancee...

STRANGER: No, no: better alone than in bad company.

LILA: It's better if I don't talk to you. You make me mad.

They begin to set the tables. Lila sings song to herself while the Stranger looks at her as if he were hatching a plan.

LILA: The treasure chest of my imagining
how black and ever darkening
it knows each pain and sorrow
that stirs within my marrow:
and I am left here all alone
so terrified of my dark zone

STRANGER: Bravo! You sing like an angel.

LILA: I'm no angel.

STRANGER: But, not a monster either are you?

LILA: Who knows ...

STRANGER: Oh, now I'm scared! By the way, aren't you afraid of the monster?

LILA: Me? Why should I be? I've never hurt anyone!

STRANGER: Well, no, but monsters aren't so finicky ... A nice looking young filly like you, all by her lonesome ... because you manage this place all by yourself, don't you...

LILA: I thought we said we weren't going to ask any questions.

STRANGER: And when did we say that?

LILA: I ah, ... I thought I heard you say ... That's why for a couple of days now the hunters seem to have disappeared.

STRANGER: They've all gone hunting for the monster?

LILA: Fat chance! Fear would have made them wet their beds... Oh, sure, real brave when they have to shoot some poor skylark, genuine heroes when they can put their hands ups some skirt, but when a monster's around, they're all in their beds with their heads under the pillow, and maybe with mommy, a rolling pin at the ready, standing guard by the door. You call those men! They've flown off just like their birds! (She laughs crazily)

STRANGER: I'm here though. I haven't flown away. Neither I nor my dicky bird... You've stopped laughing? Did I say something I shouldn't have? One allusion too many, a bit heavy-handed, perhaps?

LILA: You're not from around here. You're just passing through. Why should the monster pick on you who have nothing to do with it.

STRANGER: If it's a monster, it's probably crazy! Don't you think? And there's no reasoning with the mad, my dear!

LILA: He might be crazy, but there must be some reason to his madness.

STRANGER: And what do you know about it?

LILA: Feminine intuition.

STRANGER: So, you're defending him?

LILA: Who, me? Not a chance! I'm just saying that crazy people aren't always monsters. On the contrary, they can often become great artists, like Cezanne or that other one, that famous guy who cut off his ear.

STRANGER: It's all a matter of channelling the madness into an artistic context, even if the risk in that is to reduce art to the prerogative of a few crazy people who appoint themselves the vanguard of the mental Armageddon facing the human race.

LILA: I couldn't say. Nor would I be able tabling ... Entschuldigung! Pardon me, of setting the table... I mean, let's change the subject, if you don't mind.

STRANGER: Alright, let's talk about us, then. About our business, in the intimacy of this hour before dawn.

LILA: Don't start having bizarre fantasies.

STRANGER: Who? Me?

LILA: Yes, you. You precisely. Where do you think you're going with these allusions of yours, and not very subtle ones at that?!

STRANGER: Nowhere, I swear. I'm a serious type of guy.

LILA: Look! For me you're just some Mister Nobody who stopped for a coffee.

STRANGER: Which I still haven't had. And I'm being tied to the galley; work, slave! And not a word, button up! Look, I've already set two tables. Are you going to put in a good word for me with the boss, if you can?

LILA: I'm the owner.

STRANGER: Oh! So this is your resort then ... Well, well, well! A good catch!

LILA: My parents are dead. I have no friends and no relatives. I've been left all alone. And I like it that way just fine. I'm a little frightened at night, sure. Otherwise I make out quite well. Even with my income taxes. I don't need anyone, not even an accountant, see?

STRANGER: My, aren't you clever! But... pardon my curiosity, you're quite young ... your dear ones? An orphan? And how did it happen. A tragedy?

LILA: Why are you so interested?

STRANGER: Let me guess, please. A silly traffic accident caused by - presumably - speeding and low tire pressure. Hm?

LILA: How do you know that?

STRANGER: Well, I just guessed, but the statistics do back me up - most deaths are in fact caused by traffic accidents. Did I get it right?

LILA: (Sarcastic) Bravo!

STRANGER: I wonder why the pressure in the tires was low. It couldn't have been an oversight on the part of your dearly departed father. Isn't it true that daddy was always a stickler for detail and that he always checked his tires when he filled up with gas?

LILA: Stop it! You're always sticking your nose into what's none of your business.

STRANGER: And your adoptive parents, who so wanted a daughter but who couldn't have children, and here you come onto the scene, with your blond pig-tails, of course!, didn't they die in a tragic accident? A gas leak?

LILA: Exactly, a tragic accident.

STRANGER: And your fiancé, didn't he perish in a mountaineering mishap the day after he deflowered you? Or, if you'll pardon the leading pun, was his fatal fall-us due to a Freudian slip?

LILA: What is it that you want from me?

STRANGER: Nothing, nothing. Don't get so upset. I just wanted to point out that you've simply been unlucky, very unlucky. Perhaps too unlucky. But, in spite of the tragedies that have dogged you, notwithstanding the terrible moral blows of which you have been the victim, you've pulled yourself together, you've managed to go on all alone, and we are now dealing with a professional, an entrepreneur with all her papers in order, a capitalist-genius! Congratulations!

LILA: We, who is we?

STRANGER: The royal "we".

LILA: Well, Your Majesty, please be seated. I'll make the coffee.

STRANGER: Ah, finally! And the croissants?

LILA: Please. One thing at a tie! *(She starts going towards the counter but bumps into the suitcase)*

STRANGER: Careful!

LILA: Scheisse! I almost broke my neck. What do you mean by putting

your suitcase down in the shadows? I'll put it in the closet for you, it's in the way here...
STRANGER: No, please!
LILA: Gosh, it's heavy.
STRANGER: Please, handle it with care ... slowly ...
LILA: I'm not even going to touch it... you move it yourself, if you can.
STRANGER: (He puts the suitcase under the table) There, now it won't bother you any more.
LILA: Is it filled with rocks? It must weigh ... a ton...
STRANGER: Rocks, exactly. How did you guess?
LILA: Are you making fun of me?
STRANGER: You're the one who said rocks.
LILA: Yes, but not seriously.
STRANGER: What if I told you I'm a geologist and that in this suitcase I have rock samples; would you believe me?
LILA: No!
STRANGER: And you would be right. No. No rocks!
LILA: What, then?
STRANGER: Top secret.

LILA: And you've come to get lost smack dab in the middle of these mountains forgotten by God and the devil?

STRANGER: Not by the devil, I'll guarantee you that. He never forgets anything or anyone!

LILA: You know you're pretty weird!

STRANGER: Really? And am I cheeky?

LILA: At this hour, in the shadow, an unusual apparition, you can't deny that. Never before seen in these parts. You wouldn't by chance be the ...

STRANGER: The monster? Why not?

LILA: Don't be offended, now ... O.K.?

STRANGER: Goodness, no! I'm not the type to be offended, in fact ...

LILA: In fact, you're flattered by it.

STRANGER: Exactly. But I would like to hear your unbiased opinion about me: who am I?

LILA: How should I know?

STRANGER: A monster, yes. But that's too simple.

LILA: How do you mean?

STRANGER: All strangers are, in the very nature of things, a bit weird. And a monster is precisely the person who doesn't fit the norm and ends up being odd, right? Ambiguous, a bit kooky or, if we really want to be honest, repulsive. Is this what you feel about me, maybe unconsciously?

LILA: I don't know.

STRANGER: Come on, speak up. No holds barred. I'm not very sensitive. On the contrary, I'm interested in your impartial, even if perhaps somewhat superficial, opinion...

LILA: I repeat. I don't know. I haven't known you long enough

STRANGER: What's to know? Don't you see me? Don't you hear me?

LILA: (Annoyed) What are you talking about?

STRANGER: Nothing, nothing at all...

LILA: There, that's better.

STRANGER: Or everything.

LILA: Starting again.

STRANGER: I would like to know what you really think of me ... Come on, make an effort!

LILA: Well, if you really insist, here goes. Your eyes give off a kind of strange glow, as if they were lit up.

STRANGER: Lit up, my eyes? Are you sure?

LILA: Yes. They attract and repel me at once like a lighthouse indicating the harbour is nearby yet warning of dangerous shoals.

STRANGER: Listen to that? We're waxing poetic! With images! Indeed, using metaphors, even!

LILA: Look, I can't find words to explain myself any better...

STRANGER: Oh, I'll lend you the words, if you want, just like I've done up till now.

LILA: You ...? Don't make me laugh.

STRANGER: Laugh on, if you wish.

LILA: Look, you're crazy!

STRANGER: Yes, fit to be tied! And you're not telling me the whole truth.

LILA: What truth?

STRANGER: Come on, wouldn't you like to open up to me, you little slut?

He grabs one of her arms and squeezes tightly, hurting her. With a jerk she manages to free herself.

LILA: Fuck off!

Once again he's at her, squeezes her tightly.

STRANGER: I love it when you swear. It gets me all excited.

LILA: Go jerk off, then! And let go of me!

STRANGER: Not yet. I want to hear you yelling first...

LILA: You're hurting me.

STRANGER: Aw, I'm so sorry!

LILA: You're nails are too long, you'll make me bleed.
STRANGER: It's the fault of your flesh. You have such soft flesh!
LILA: By God!

At the word "God" he lets her go immediately.

STRANGER: Sorry. I was joking, just joking.
LILA: Some joke. You almost shattered my arm.
STRANGER: Oh, it's just a little scratch ... I'll tell my manicurist to trim my claws, O.K.?
LILA: Tell your manicurist to send you to the devil for me. (To herself) What a piece of shit!
STRANGER: I'll be sure to do that.
LILA: Don't mention it. And don't you dare touch me again.
STRANGER: Right.
LILA: I should call the police. You almost attacked me!
STRANGER: Almost, only almost.
LILA: Why, would you have gone any further? Aren't the marks you left on my arm enough? Look, look!
STRANGER: Don't be upset. It was just a moment, a moment of insanity. I admit it, I should have restrained myself, I shouldn't have lost

control, but it's also a bit your own fault...

LILA: Mine?

STRANGER: Your perfume.

LILA: But I haven't put on any perfume yet.

STRANGER: But you smell of you, don't you see?

LILA: No, I'd rather not understand.

STRANGER: You smell of flesh ... young flesh!

LILA: Listen, from now on, keep your distance. Please! At least three paces away ... (she counts them) One, two, three ... Agreed?

STRANGER: Verstanden... Promise!

LILA: And the way you looked at me! You should have seen yourself: your pupils were dilated and filled with blood like ...

STRANGER: An animal?

LILA: Exactly. How did ... ?

STRANGER: How did I guess?

LILA: Yes. You're frightening me.

STRANGER: Finally!

LILA: Oh! You find it amusing do you?! Fine! That'll teach me to trust the first person to come along!

STRANGER: Listen. I'm sorry I frightened you. Seriously!

LILA: And you think that'll get you off. Just saying you're sorry?

STRANGER: Why not? Nothing really happened... Nothing serious, I mean.

LILA: And the scratches? Did I dream those up?

STRANGER: Of course not.

LILA: You see? I'm right. Real, grave matters have transpired; facts which are unequiv...

STRANGER: The claws of a cat that didn't want to be held any more. That's all!

LILA: And you would be the cat?

STRANGER: Why not? Being a cat, suits me fine.

LILA: And I'm the mouse, I take it?

STRANGER: A stimulating idea. I hadn't thought of it. Good thing you're here!

LILA: You'll end up in jail.

STRANGER: And the witnesses to prove, corroborate, etcetera, etcetera?

LILA: What about my word?

STRANGER: Your ... what? (He laughs) Oh, I see, well of course, your word!!! La dee da!

LILA: You're the sly one, aren't you? You always know how to wriggle your way out of a tough spot. You're an expert at assault as well as legal niceties so you don't have to face the music. Men like you should be castrated at birth! Or drowned or quartered, damn you all!

STRANGER: Wow! That's the monster's voice, you know, lurking within you? Careful not to stoke him too much! He might peek out and ... boo!

LILA: Monster? Me? And you? Who are you? What have you got in the suitcase? The tools of the trade, I'll bet. Spikes, chains, tenterhooks... My God, what am I saying!

STRANGER: Why do you want to know? Female curiosity?

LILA: Have you got something to hide?

STRANGER: And if I confessed that I've got a woman's corpse cut up into little pieces? What would you do? Would you call for help?

LILA: Damn right!

STRANGER: But we're quite isolated here, on the edge of the forest. And the wind would sweep away the sound of your voice to, who knows where, to what deserted gully...You poor little thing! I really feel for you. I'm tempted to console you ... in my own way, of course!

LILA: (Frightened) What...are you serious?

STRANGER: What difference does is make whether it's real or imagined? Besides, isn't that what you really wanted from me?

LILA: Me?

STRANGER: Yes, you, of course you, with your irritating morbidness.

LILA: Morbid, me? You're the one who's morbid!

STRANGER: Was I the one who asked you what you keep in your refrigerator? No, so I'm not the one who's morbid. For all I care, next to your beef stew, you could be keeping the corpse of a new-born. What do I know about your past, hmm?

LILA: The pressure is building.

STRANGER: In me too. And it's killing me! And it's all your fault, and that of your ferocious subconscious. It'scontagious, you know?

LILA: The pressure in the espresso machine is building. Mein Gott! In five minutes I can make you your damn coffee. Und fertig, Schluss. You leave just as you came; vanish into thin air, nothingness, into ambiguity. OK?

STRANGER: That's fine with me. I can't wait to get out of here.

LILA: Five minutes, just five...

STRANGER: An eternity.

LILA: Not at all. It's an instant.

STRANGER: Three hundred seconds, to be exact.

LILA: And you call that an eternity?

STRANGER: Time is a subjective construct. Sometimes it passes quickly, at other times it seems interminable. It doesn't always go by at the same rate. Or in the same direction. Sometimes it goes forwards, sometimes backwards. It depends. They call it the arrow of time, because in fact it follows the evolution of the universe, projected into the future and, in the opposite direction, into the past. The theory of eternal return, for example... Nietzsche! What a marvel he was! A bit whacko, but he had balls, he did...

LILA: Who are you trying to hoodwink? You take me for an idiot? I'm a small town girl, granted, but inside, inside me there's...

STRANGER: A daemon?

LILA: The devil!?

STRANGER: If you insist...

LILA: No, you're the one who's insisting a bit much, do you hear me? You've understood that I'm afraid of you and you're having fun at my expense. You're a sadist, a maniac, a monster!

STRANGER: Just because my nails are a bit long?

LILA: I have them too! I can defend myself, don't you fool yourself!

STRANGER: In fact it seems that the devil was born female, and then, through a trick of nature, acquired testicles. He represents the so-called woman with a dick or, to be less vulgar, as our friend Freud said, the phallic woman. As though you, if you allow me, had a clitoris the size of a penis. There you have it. That is what the Lord of the Nether World or Darkness is, an upside down cock. The classical serpent biting its own tail... (laughing)

LILA: Die listige Schlange ... The cunning serpent!

STRANGER: Precisely. Mozart. (sings the aria from The Magic Flute) ...

Der listigen Schlange
zum Opfer erkoren ...

By the way, do you believe in the devil?

LILA: In this day and age it would be ridiculous to believe in him.

STRANGER: But it could be dangerous not to believe in him...very dangerous.

LILA: In your opinion...he exists?

STRANGER: In my opinion something, somewhere does exist. I can't tell you where, however...

LILA: Maybe at the centre of the earth...

STRANGER: Centre of the earth! Perfect. That's where the elements are in their pure state, like the devil, like hell, primordial symbols of our erupting and volcanic imagination.

LILA: Mein Gott! You're so puzzling.

STRANGER: Let's just say enigmatic, Fräulein.

LILA: Can you tell my mother tongue is German? In Italian I sort of limp a bit, sometimes, I know I do.

STRANGER: You speak Italian very well. But you think in German. Like Faust.

LILA: And what does that mean?

STRANGER: It means that Germans have always felt a morbid attraction to the Evil One.

LILA: There... I thought I'd seen you before, heard your voice, as if your image and your words had sprung from me, as if they were a projection of my anxieties, an incarnation of what really frightens me.

STRANGER: And what is it that really frightens you? Come on, fess up, I can't stand it any longer!

LILA: Death, perhaps... No, I'm even more afraid of suffering.

STRANGER: And of sex, that "sweetest and most powerful dominator of my profoundest thoughts, terrible but dear gift from heaven" of which Leopardi speaks, isn't that right?

LILA: I'm telling you one more time to stay where you belong.

STRANGER: Good Lord, but you're sensitive! Do you suspect, know?

LILA: It's fear, just fear.

STRANGER: Oh no, but you mustn't. After all, I'm not as bad as I look, really.

LILA: It's as if you were privy to the darkest recesses of my imaginings, hidden even from me, and which sometimes drag me by the hair, assailing me with images I would rather not see, with things I would rather not do ... I can't explain myself any better than that.

STRANGER: Oh, you're explaining yourself very well. You know what they say, a word to the wise ...

LILA: Your facial features, they... seem ... familiar to me; your voice, I recognize it as if it were my own. (she hesitates) Strange ... (she looks at him) Have we met before?

STRANGER: In dreams, perhaps. Why not? (Obscenely) I love to penetrate young women like you in their dreams!

LILA: You're playing with fire!

STRANGER: So are you, you know!

LILA: (After a tense pause) So let's not joke around with these things.

STRANGER: You're right. Dreams, especially nightmares during a full moon, are a risky business, off limits. Access denied to unauthorized personnel. Am I right? Private property!

LILA: (Laughs) Beware of dog.

STRANGER: The three-headed dog, good! How did you guess?

LILA: Three heads? (Jokingly) Bow-wow!

STRANGER: Yes, there you go! Bow-wow says Pluto's dog which guards the entrance to Hell. Bow-wow! Bow-wow

LILA: (It dies in her throat) Bow ...wo...

He's begun jumping around on all fours, like a dog.

STRANGER: Bow-wow! Bow-wow!

LILA: (Frightened) Tha ... That's enough, you're scaring me! Stop it! Enough!

STRANGER: The bad thing about dreams is that they can come true as if by ...as if by ... magic!

LILA: Or by sadism.

STRANGER: Are you mad at me.

LILA: No ... I mean, yes! You shouldn't have pranced about like a mad dog. You shouldn't have done it so well. You really seemed to be a rabid dog.

STRANGER: No, just a little black poodle. That's more than enough.

LILA: Poodle my eye!

STRANGER: Well, maybe a bot Mephistophelian.

LILA: Please, don't start again with your arcane references ... (surprised at herself) What a strange word ... What does arcane mean?

STRANGER: You're the one who said it.

LILA: Yes, I said it, but I'm not the one who expressed it, in my thoughts.

STRANGER: How do you like that? Who could it have been, then ... it sounded like your voice to me.

LILA: I'm just a simple girl, what do I know about such expressions ... and in Italian even ... My mother tongue is German, after all ... No, no. It couldn't have been me who thought it!

STRANGER: Who could it have been, then? The devil?

LILA: You put that word inside me, on my tongue: you made me say it.

STRANGER: How did I manage that?

LILA: I don't know. You're contagious. You've lured me into this dialectical trap... there you are, another word that's not mine ... and I'll never be able to get out of this cerebral trap ... Help! I'm being held prisoner by a monster.

STRANGER: Internal or external? Real or imaginary? Concrete or phantasmagoric? You have to touch to believe...

LILA: No, don't touch me!

STRANGER: You really do have the devil in you.

LILA: I won't play! I won't play this game, you bastard!

STRANGER: You'll play, you'll play! Don't play the coy one with me, like Marguerite ... (he looks at her as if he's trying to hypnotize her; her face is lit up as if by a strange reflection)

LILA: Who's Marguerite?

STRANGER: An old acquaintance of mine. One of the many girlfriends I've got lying around. A sailor has a girl in every port; it's a known fact. But poor Marguerite, unfortunately, is gone: lost forever, dead and buried! Too bad for her...

LILA: And how did she die?

STRANGER: From a terrible disease: love! ... In the sense that she made love, that is screwed, fucked, copulated (she got laid). To make a long story short, she coupled carnally with a monster.

LILA: A monster?

STRANGER: Yes! Of flesh and bone (maybe more bone than flesh!). A decrepit old man disguised as a young stud with a cock like this! ... And a heart no bigger that this.... Get the picture?

LILA: And she loved him even though he was such a slimy, repulsive creature?

STRANGER: Monsters are like that, you love them or hate them, there's no alternative. And both at once: totally, desperately, until one reaches the end of the road or until the redemption - usually not very likely, because the lower one falls, the harder it is to climb back up - of the monster.

LILA: Why are you looking at me is if you were the monster?

STRANGER: Don't pay it any mind.

LILA: You almost blinded me ... and I shouldn't pay it any mind?!

STRANGER: It's only a reflection of the moon which still comes and goes alternating mystery with clarity among the clouds of night shorn by the wind.

LILA: How poetic you are! You make me puke.

STRANGER: Well, when you've got to, you've got to, my dear. Besides, everything is so confused in these warrens of time, as though nothing existed and, at the same time, could exist, even ... Do you understand? Even?

LILA: Oh, no!

STRANGER: Oh, yes! So poetry helps to capture the more essential nuances, to sublimate everything, so the chaos in which we are immersed won't become trivia, where excitement barely manages to produce a bit of enjoyment and the drawn out little orgasm of some snot-nosed school girls first finger job.

LILA: Schämen Sie sich! You should be ashamed of yourself!

STRANGER: Fortunately, however, there's poetry. And with it our conscience is salved, the ear remains unpolluted, the tongue need not speak of what ails it. And everything is solved by a super-galactic, linguistic wank. There, happy now?

LILA: What do you care? Anyway, I'm not speaking to you any more. You're too vulgar ...

STRANGER: Don't be afraid. Soon the sun will come up. And everything will end.

LILA: Really?

STRANGER: Yes, yes. You'll see. The bad dreams will evaporate.

LILA: And you'll be on your way again? I'll heave a sigh of relief, I can tell you.

STRANGER: You make me out to be a nightmare, thanks. That's nice of you. However, I'll agree. If and when the sun rises, I'll fade away. I promise. And a promise is a promise, at least for me.

LILA: If and when the sun rises?

STRANGER: I'm speaking hypothetically.

LILA: In the sense that the sun might never rise again?

STRANGER: Oh no, do you take me for an idiot? Do you think I don't know that sooner or later the sun has to come up as it has for hundreds of millions of years.

LILA: What do you mean, then?

STRANGER: That one of us may not make it to sunrise. Had that never occurred to you?

LILA: But if there are only a few minutes till ... Are you a murderer?
STRANGER: My dear! The worst killer, our worst enemy, is fate. It's fate that's in charge. What does it have to do with me? I obey. I obey and struggle. Sometimes I don't understand, but I adapt. So, I succumb, if succumb I must. And the same goes for you.
LILA: Fate?
STRANGER: Certainly. For if, for example, fate has decreed that in ten seconds you must die - maybe of heartache - can you object? Rebel? Defend yourself? Try it! Come on, let me see you try ... Struggle, squirm, fly into a rage. Go ahead, hit me, hit me here, I'm fate. Scratch me, resist! See?   You   can't.

LILA: Me? In ten seconds?
STRANGER: ... ten, nine (look how time flies sometimes!) ... six, five ... (what is a second? It seem like nothing, but in one second are born and die million, billions of microorganisms!) ... three, two, one, zero! Do you feel O.K.?
LILA: Yes, I think so... I hope so!
STRANGER: Well fate hasn't yet decided what your fate is going to be. Besides, one can't force its hand in the opposite direction. Because you see, the Fates, who spin out the lives of human beings from Hell, are quite strapped for production time. Well, there are only three of them for

the entire human race! You do see the problem!!

LILA: I'd really like to smash my fist in your ugly, monstrous mug.

STRANGER: Go ahead, make fun. Would you prefer me to vanish like a dream when you wake up: you rub your eyes, have a coffee and ... Oh, by the way ... the coffee?

LILA: If you stop blathering!

STRANGER: Well, you see, unfortunately for you, I'm not just a dream. Maybe a fairy tale come true, but a dream...

LILA: God, I can't take it any more!

STRANGER: (He pulls back) No, please. Don't take His name in vain. Have some respect! If not for Him, at least for me!

LILA: Sometimes I seem to catch a glimmer of the truth, but then it slips away again, vanishes, and I get lost and don't know what road to take inside me to get out again...

STRANGER: Do you really want to know? Think about it carefully...

LILA: I don't know. It depends on what.

STRANGER: What's being agitated in your cerebral organ; and that emerges in bits and pieces from the abyss of your consciousness like a subterranean wave breaking on the shore of you Ego spraying jets of incandescent lava...

LILA: Your ps... psyche (another word I didn't know till now) is more

contorted than mine.
STRANGER: Contorted in the extreme, I'll grant you. Try to undo the slip-knot of my consciousness and you too will end up inextricably bound to the anchor which drags me about on the bottom, in the immense vortex in which, in your dream, you've just glimpsed ... the Beast!
LILA: Damned Beast! Damn you!

STRANGER: It's better that way, believe me - and I hope you follow my advice - keep yourself under control. All of oneself under lock and key, like in a convent.
LILA: Or like what's inside the suitcase. I'm really curious to...
STRANGER: Oh no, don't open it, don't ever open it; think of that suitcase as your soul. What is inside, once it's out in the open, could be destroyed. Who can say what ugliness could spring from it...
LILA: From my soul?
STRANGER: Inside you, you have a kind of fireworks factory in which a single spark can unleash a chain reaction with disastrous consequences. A Pandora's box, believe me.
LILA: You're scaring me to death.
STRANGER: And I beg you not to be frightened. It's not worth it. We're sitting on an atom bomb? So what? As long as it doesn't explode, we can even make love on it, if it we're so inclined. We have a monster

inside us? As long as it stays hunched up in some corner and doesn't break your balls (sorry!) with its bestial barking. Anyway, what is existence, when all is said and done: a fragment careening wildly by for a tiny bit of time through the darkness of eternity? Why get so upset over it? It's for such a short time, after all. Listen! Enjoy your life as long as you can. And don't think about it any more.

LILA: What shouldn't I think about?

STRANGER: What do you mean? About the Beast!

LILA: Sometimes it howls, yells like a hyena maddened by pangs of hunger. At other times it bares its teeth, ready to strike. Easy for you to say, don't think about it!

STRANGER: Make believe that your mind is like my suitcase, alright? That is, empty, until we - me in my suitcase and you in your mind - put something in it. Am I right?

LILA: Maybe...maybe I'm not up to snuff, up to your level...a bad girl, spiteful...that's all I am...what do you expect from me? How do you expect me to compete with a...with a...

STRANGER: With a devil?

LILA: Yes. Yes. I'm sorry.

STRANGER: Nothing to apologize for. Everyone sees things his own way. And if you see me as a devil, then fine, I'm a devil. Happy?

LILA: I wish I'd never met you. I wish your car had broken down far away from here. I wish you hadn't seen the light and thought I was about to open up. I wish the hunters were coming for breakfast...

STRANGER: You're forgetting something in this nauseating wish list of yours. (He imitates her delivery) I wish the monster didn't exist or that, even though he exists, he hadn't committed his atrocities. Right?
LILA: You're really determined to scare me to death, aren't you?
STRANGER: Scared? You?
LILA: Yes, yes, me! Frightened of myself. Of what I've done or of what I might do and will do, that I know I'll end up doing. That's when the bottled up anxiety bursts free in me and spills out like foam when you shake a bottle of beer, and it covers things, people, everything!
STRANGER: Those are the symptoms, the roots of the evil lurking within you: the Beast. It would be best if you could somehow intuit without knowing, since complete, full knowledge of oneself can also lead - it almost inevitably does lead - to the bottomless pit of despair. It's a difficult thing, of course, subconscious intuition is, but it's still possible. Understand without knowing...with the end in view, of course, of destroying the animal we are without destroying the soul, smashing it into tiny pieces for nothing. How, you may well ask? Well, that's why I'm here. Let me concentrate for a moment and you'll see!

LILA: (After a pause) You're thinking of a naked woman? Hey, that woman is me! And I'm touching myself, I don't want to, you pig! What am I doing in your thoughts?

STRANGER: Everyone concentrates as he sees fit. Some while smoking a cigarette and some...now look, don't barge in on my erotic fantasies. Surely I'm free to...

LILA: How could I possibly have looked inside you! Or was it inside me?

|**STRANGER:** Silence!

LILA: Oh my God! You're thinking inside me! You're thinking about me inside me!

STRANGER: Shuuuut uuuuup!

He struggles to concentrate. But this effort produces a series of strange, paranormal effects, such as noises, bright lights, images which flit rapidly across the walls, shadows and finally a brutal scene, a disturbing coupling of two monsters from which is born a horrible baby monster.

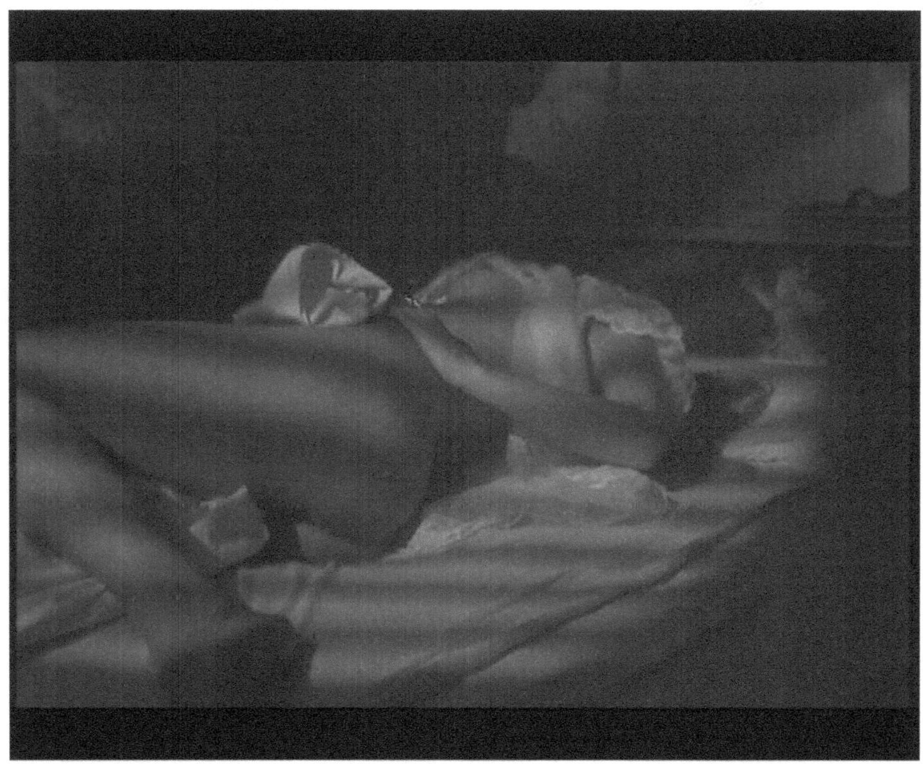

STRANGER: See? Did you hear? Intuit? Are you satisfied? Did you come?

LILA: And I'm supposed to have... Inside...of me.. this...abomination?

STRANGER: Even worse? I've touched on the odd odd bauble, en passant, as it were! Let's say the best of what's going on inside you! Goethe would have written hundreds of pages (my how he did go on with the homunculus and the beautiful soul!) Me, I just get right down to the nitty gritty. Very few words. Let the facts speak for themselves. You can read about it all you want, but until you get your hands filthy, you just don't believe it...

LILA: I'm so defenceless against myself...

STRANGER: And that makes you cry? Don't you think you're overdoing it a bit? It's certainly true that there's no greater evil than that which springs from within us, but, there's a remedy for everything, believe me.

LILA: No, I won't believe you.

STRANGER: Don't despair. After all, the gaping pit you have inside you is no darker or more barbaric than those of your ilk. If you dig deep into man, you'll always find a stone age man in there, don't you know? How is it, I ask myself, that you haven't made giant strides in...how many is it now ...three thousand years of history? And you've remained so primitive, cave-man-like, bestial?

LILA: Not me. Not me, or at least I didn't know I was like what you're saying.

STRANGER: And wouldn't it have been better to go on not knowing, not seeing, not feeling, like the Three Little Monkeys? If the Ego doesn't hear what the Id says, the Id doesn't see what Conscience does and the Conscience keeps quiet about what the other two are doing, that would be Heaven I tell you, believe me!

LILA: I'm having an anxiety attack. Stop it!

STRANGER: Still, the ancestral fears which materialize in your thoughts - which in turn become concrete in images which become flesh and give life to carnal activities (no matter how you slice it, we always end up here, with the flesh, which may be weak, but oh so sweet!) - I've lost my train of thought. What was I saying...?

LILA: My ancestral fears...

STRANGER: Right, exactly, they've been blown up by the darkness like monstrous shadows projected on the walls of your Ego. If an ant crosses the lens of a projector, on the screen you'll see a prehistoric-looking monster, a creature from hell. And you'll believe, naively, that you've seen the devil in person. But in fact, what was it really, hm?

LILA: Nothing.

STRANGER: Right, nothing! And so it is with nightmares, which seem unbearable while you're asleep and which, once you're awake, you want to erase from your mind. But what do they in fact represent, if not a small fraction, a few seconds of our nightly nirvana? And should we wreck our lives for a few tenths of a second during which the mind runs wild, builds up to a dizzying speed and burns the asphalt before putting on the inhibiting brakes?

LILA: I don't know... I don't know what to do.

STRANGER: You've just said it. Nothing. Forget about the outlines suggested by some fleeting lights, whispers of the infinite, abstract images thrust up against the leaden sky of the soul which, at times seems to want to snuff you out in the cradle (ah yes, I too was a child once, and I still remember the anxiety filled days, when the awareness of oneself, the soul, was an empty container, an switch turned off!), and at other times, instead, it has the power of raising us above the celestial spheres because of a spiritual vortex it possesses, a process of internal sublimation. A bit like wine which matures over time, and is transformed from juice to nectar, at once divine and demonic, given that there is no god without a devil, and vice-versa.

LILA: As long as this wine doesn't turn to vinegar.

STRANGER: It's up to us to prevent it, that's the point.

LILA: Now you'll have to tell me how you can get inside my mind.

STRNANGER: Oh, no, no. What do you take me for? First of all, I wouldn't be able to. And then, what reason would I have for doing such a thing?

LILA: So, what happens now?

STRANGER: You're simply thinking what I'm saying out loud. You think it simultaneously with me and think that I'm sucking away your ideas, like a vampire, like a leech, (he tries to kiss her on the neck) like a pacifier.

LILA: (She pulls away) And?

STRANGER: There's no and. I say things which are down to earth, quite banal, that you can understand. You believe you're thinking what I'm thinking and that I'm thinking what you're thinking. But only because I'm expressing some rather obvious concepts, UNIVERSAL ONES! That is, valid for all mankind.

LILA: Well, lucky you.

STRANGER: Don't worry. I'm not as diabolical as I seem.

LILA: Maybe... But you limp.

STRANGER: Me? Really? I never noticed. I'll have my hooves looked at.

LILA: And also your left foot is bigger than your right one. It seems to be bursting out of its shoe!

STRANGER: It's the foot I use to I push the brakes of inhibition. Maybe I've been a little heavy-footed in the last little while... (He takes off his shoe and exhibits a monster of a foot)

LILA: But, you've got a goat's hoof there instead of a foot.
STRANGER: So? (He quickly puts the shoe back on) You're not racist, are you? You've got something against those who are a little different? Look in the mirror. You've got an ugly spot on your neck. But out of courtesy, I haven't pointed it out to you till now. Here's what we'll do. When you get yourself looked at by a dermatologist for that growth I'll go to a shoemaker for my shoe.
LILA: You're quite right to treat me like a ninny. I must have made a mistake.
STRANGER: Well, there's not much light... And your imagination played a stupid trick on you. Still, you know, you see monsters everywhere. It's an obsession! Even in me, who, till now have behaved rather like a gentleman (aside from the marks on your arm, an excess of animal zeal which I fall prey to from time to time), even though I could have taken advantage of the situation to satisfy my desires, if I had any, and I'm not saying I don't. But it seems to me that I've been able to keep them under control rather well, wouldn't you say?

LILA: (Nervous, moves to the window) Where is that sun? This is such a cold night and it's lasting forever!

Without being seen, he guzzles down a couple of bottles of schnapps, fills his mouth with anything he can put his hands on, he steals some change from the cash register, he picks his nose and sticks the snot under the counter. He farts and smells it enthusiastically. All the while Lila is drumming her fingers on the window.

STRANGER: You see, eternity is an abstraction, yet another vague product of the mind which in its limited and contingent nature, creates itself and an ad hoc, hypothetical, non-existent infinity. As if the infinite were a simple succession of geometric (or mathematical) points that one can get to and put in one's pocket, as kind of golden ass that continues shitting gold coins! But it's not like that at all! The mistake lies in thinking of eternity in terms of quantity and not of quality. The instant is eternal, not all the instants put together. To reach infinity means to be able say to the Instant, the Moment, like Faust "stop, it's beautiful!" and not "how boring, hurry up and get it over with!". Take me, for example. I too came by here drawn by an irresistible force - the desire to have a coffee. I stopped. And I've been waiting forever!

LILA: Where are you from?

STRANGER: You really want to know? I come from a place you don't know... and, I'm sure, that you don't want to know. So let it go, will you, it's better that way. Much better for you.

LILA: From across the border?

STRANGER: Much farther than that. Too far, perhaps.

LILA: So mysterious!

STRANGER: What's life without a little mystery?

LILA: Nothing. You're right.

STRANGER: Exactly, food without salt... Now, however, I've got to take a piss... May I? Where's the loo?

LILA: Down the back, on the left... Wait, it's locked. I have to get you the key. Damn! (She rummages through a drawer) Where did I put it?

STRANGER: Hurry up, my prostate's a bit bonkers because of my frequent and humungous erections.

LILA: I can't find it...(she searches frantically) I keep it locked so addicts won't sneak it... drugs, unfortunately, have come even to these parts.. those poor youngsters!

STRANGER: Look, who gives a damn?

LILA: Here it is, I've found it...

STRANGER: (Grabs the key from her) Give me that... (he goes in the wrong direction)

LILA: On the left, I said. Links!

STRANGER: (Fumbling nervously with the lock) Dammit, I ended up in the kitchen...following the smell, you know? In this lodge the burners and the pots stink more than the toilets.

LILA: (Alone) Alone with that madman! He says such things... brr. It gives me goose bumps! (She peers out the window) And it just would be today that nobody shows up, not even those who come for their "usual" coffee (with a snort, oh my, shhh! Mustn't say such things so early in the morning). Usually at this time they're knocking on the window and they have me pass the tray out to them so they don't have to take off their jackets and tie up their dogs (I don't allow those salivating beasts in here)... This morning, however, no one, niemand, as if...as if the monster...that's all I needed, the monster! As if business wasn't bad enough already...

The door to the washroom is thrown open. Lila doesn't notice and keeps looking out, waiting for someone to arrive. He is intent on urinating. But it's a diabolical piss, its sound rising till it becomes the roar of a waterfall. Then the flushing toilet becomes a frightful vortex. Lila is annoyed by the thundering animal noises.

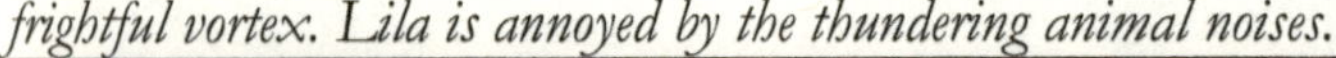

LILA: You've been locked up there for some time, now. Are you feeling all right?
STRANGER: Is it day yet?
LILA: Not yet... (to herself) This is odd...
STRANGER: Well, I'm very well, then, don't fret. I've just got a lot of

buttons to do up... my clothes are a bit old-fashioned... A kind of costume, like that of a ring-master I've been told, but I like it just fine. And it's very comfortable, too, except when you've got to get the wee-wee out! But I don't think you have such problems ... Get back inside, you animal! Heel!
LILA: Who are you talking to?
STRANGER: A childhood friend I used to play with in my spare time. Every once in a while I dust it off, and take it out to get some air.

Meanwhile the bathroom has become engulfed in an eerie, reddish vapour rising from the toilet bowl, accompanied by strange noises: moaning, screams, screeching and flashing infernal lights. All of a sudden, having been with his back to the audience, he turns around and exhibits his true diabolic features: an ass's head with horns drip

ping with blood.

STRANGER: I am the dark side of light, he who lifts his gaze up to God and dares display the truth in all its nakedness. The God who set seven plagues on mankind, the God who commanded Abraham to offer up as sacrifice, inhuman act though it was, his first born in whom he delighted, the God who forced upon his own child, flesh of his spirit, the agony on the cross, and to hold back man's urge to attain eternity could only think of bestowing upon him one birthright: death, in exchange for life there in the hereafter which doesn't exist because there is barely a life in the here and now, you still consider Hi to be the Eternal Father (God Almighty)? Ok, then. That God is me, Baphomet, and there is no other God before me! What a crock of shit it all is! To make man's stupid mind believe that he is a creature suspended between good and evil and that he has the power to make the ultimate decision, as if he really were the one to decide. Oh, man, you're just a poor jerk whom the serpent allowed to have just one bite: you messed up your life and accepted to play this game of slaughter with the same Creator who, just like some toy put you in this garden on earth so he could bowl once in a while and knock down some

pins. Me, me, me. It's me alone who am your God! And there is no other God before me! (With a smile) Signed: Baphomet!

A howling of wolves echoes his words from which a voice can be made out.

THE LAMENT OF THE LONESOME WOLF
The man of men is the wolf no other animal is worse than he
I must nourish myself on garbage
while he shoots at whoever can fly.
In his own image God created him
but then he revealed the true face

of his soul: and into a devil
he changed himself, thinking him different from himself.
But what monsters are lurking in the dark
which aren't products of his fantasy?
The shadows on the wall are pure madness
which change reality into a manic mess.

Be careful, Lila, of the terrible monster
he has hidden himself inside you
fight it with all your being
otherwise you'll by obsessed.

LILA: (Agitated by the howling) Damned ugly beasts! They're all I needed to drive me mad with fear! When the frost comes they approach inhabited areas to rummage through the garbage in search of something to stave off their hunger. What wolves!? They've become hyenas, disgusting things, unnatural, zombies which are slimier and more repulsive than serpents! And the hungrier they are, the bolder and nastier they get; they even go so far as to challenge the hunters and try to get into houses ... they've even learned to take on vague human forms, so that at night you can just make out the difference because of their long, sharp teeth and their hairy ears... I don't trust him either. He says such strange things! His face is so ambiguous! What if he's a wolf, I mean the monster? I wonder what he really has in the suitcase.. (she drags it out into the open) Dear me, it weighs a lot! What if there really is a body inside? No, it's not possible... It would be spattered with blood... But what if they're frozen pieces placed in plastic bags...? My God! I can't stand this not knowing, I've got to know. Because if he really is a monster, a genuine monster, some kind of wolf, I might be his next victim. Who knows what's going on in its head ... Besides, what harm can it do if I just take a little peek, just to reassure myself that I'm not dealing with ... But you've got to hurry, Lila, hurry...before he comes back ...

The stranger appears, looking normal again, behind her. He surveys the scene in silence, a satisfied smirk on his face, without betraying his presence, as though he wanted Lila to start rummaging around his things. Lila snaps the two locks open and mutters...

LILA: Komisch, they're unlocked...

Then she slowly opens the lid, as if she were afraid something would jump out at her, some monstrous surprise (which is accompanied by appropriate noises). As the lid is slowly lifted, Lila's face becomes bathed in a blood-red light emanating from the

*suitcase from which also issue noxious coloured fumes. Lila stays there looking at the
frightening contents of the suitcase, which she then snaps shut with a scream.*

LILA: Noooo!
STRANGER: Well?! Did you like the show, Miss? What did you hope
you'd find in there, hm? Bouquets of roses?
LILA: The sinister light of his look...! How stupid of me not to have
understood.. What, who was hiding behind his strange words, all those
insinuations...the monster, the maniac!
STRANGER: You can also add: the psychopath! You see, I'm not
offended.
LILA: Don't touch me. Don't come any closer! Help!
STRANGER: It's your fault. You had to stick your nose into my
suitcase, and it's as if the lid had come off the conscience which served as
a cork: pop, and the champagne, the nectar of demons and gods spurted
out shaken by your pretty little hands which were soiled as though by the
seed of a monster. And now, come! Come!
LILA: How disgusting!
STRANGER: Pop, pop: look in here, look! (He forces her to look
inside the suitcase)
LILA: No, leave me alone. I'm not bad! I'm not a monster!
STRANGER: Stop, it's beautiful! Stop, it's beautiful! (Laughs)

*The Stranger pulls out a varied assortment of objects found in sex shops, putting them
on himself and forcing Lila to touch them etc. Meanwhile from the espresso machine a
dense fog begins to spew out till the stage becomes completely engulfed and slowly
disappears from view.*

STRANGER: The psyche is a mechanism under pressure. If the escape
valves are all plugged up, sooner or later it's going to undergo
degeneration. And you are degenerate!
LILA: It's not true.
STRANGER: Really? Is this not your hand-writing? Oh, this is good:
you've written a confession to yourself. Go ahead, read it.
LILA: (Reads) Dear Monster:
         Here I am, engulfed in extreme sorrow, in a suffering beyond
endurance surrounded by nothing but a painful silence. But I'm still
waiting for a sign, a message - suggested by your calls for help - that
would allow me, Acome what may, to communicate with you. I ask
myself how you can possibly live with the ghosts of your cruelty, with the

sense of guilt which you - I'm certain of it - harbour within you. I wonder whether and how you manage to shake off the anxiety and the torment - because of the bit of humanity which, in spite of everything, I still see in you - that should be assailing you. You've violated me in the most inner depth of my soul, in the deepest and truest moment of love and, obsessively, I ask myself why? I would like to look into your eyes and understand - yes, understand! - what you feel now, whether there is the desire in you to free yourself of this gesture which marks your existence, whether the sense of profound failure, the uselessness of your actions torment you, as the reality of death afflicts me. At least help me to understand, let me feel that it isn't true that you're a Amonster@, but just someone gone astray who, despite the evil committed, and for other reasons, is united to me by a common bond of suffering: the harm done to our Humanity. Don't let the silence become a tool for destroying all semblance of feeling.

Signed: a Monster named Lila.

BRIEF APPEARANCE OF BAPHOMET
(Dressed like a magician, he performs some cheap magic tricks; circus music is playing)

Take a guess at what is what
what is this and what is that!
Lend an ear, and listen well
though it seems silly as hell
to have to deal with what's been said already.
Well, then, here goes...
Often it can appear very arcane
an inkling of what man's soul may attain
yet it will seem empty to the profane
who seek to find themselves, though quite in vain,
and all full of sand their hands will remain.
What is it? What is it? What is it?
You have three seconds to give an answer
or with me yourself to hell you must commit.
One, two...three!
Why, you make laugh, I swear!
You haven't got the answer yet?
Oh, come, why it's the infinite!
But now your time is up, and it's too late
You've lost your soul; it's bound for hell's wide gate

LILA: The emptiness of my imagining
how black and ever darkening
it knows each pain and sorrow
that stirs within my marrow:
and I am left here all alone
so terrified of my dark zone.

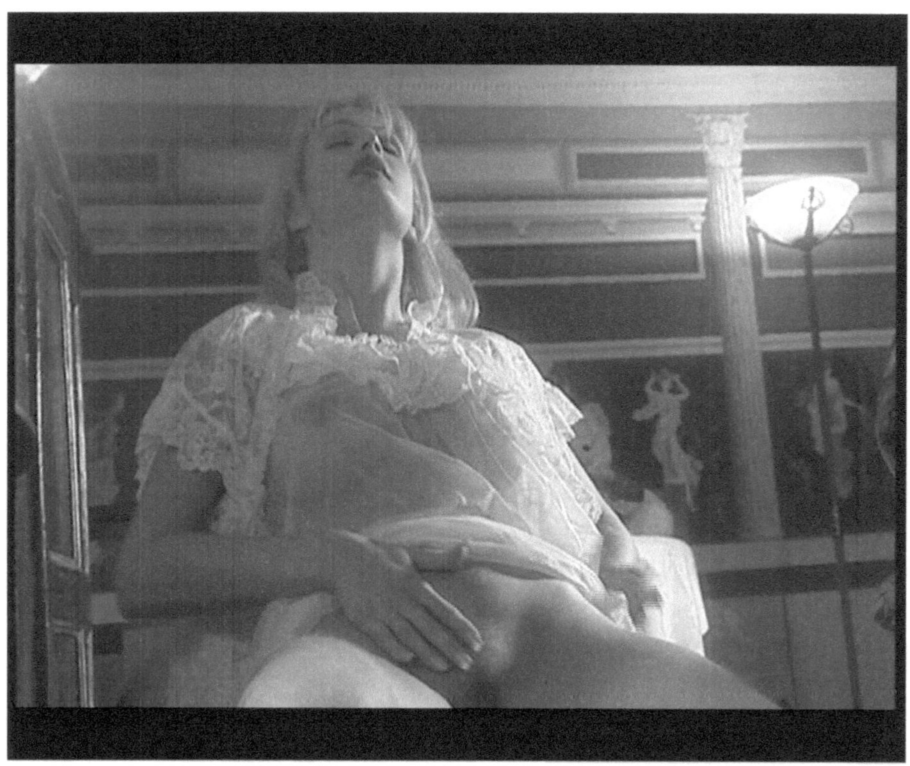

Suddenly the moon undergoes a transformation.. It turns red, grows horns and - with a series of superimposed backlit images - it's Baphomet: the Devil.

BAPHOMET-MOON: Hi, Lila!
LILA: Hi, moon,
BAPHOMET-MOON: How are you?
LILA: Lousy, as usual. Depressed.

BAPHOMENT-MOON: So I see. But whatever for? Life is so beautiful!

LILA: I'm bad. Life is a nightmare for me.

BAPHOMET-MOON: Oh, come now. Wouldn't you like to get out of here? We could go to the amusement park and go to the Monster House, for example. Wouldn't that be wonderful. Ooh Whee! It'd be a hoot!

LILA: No. You only want to make me suffer. Even more than I am!

BAPHOMET-MOON: No, no. I want to help you, to cheer you up a bit, really I do. Help you find an explanation, a solution, a way out. I'd like to alleviate your suffering, which would otherwise be truly infernal...

LILA: Please have pity, help me, I don't want to start again; keep me locked up...and throw away the key. And you, you animal, go away. Damn you!

BAPHOMET-MOON: Then I'll come to visit you. See you soon! You can't get free of yourself so easily; you can't get away from the daemon lurking inside you. He's always on his guard, trying so he can take advantage of the limits of your conscience. No, Lila, see you soon! It's fate...

The moon turns back to normal. Lila gets up suddenly, goes to the mirror and begins to make faces, to pull at her hair.

LILA: Who are you, huh? Who are you? A monster? Or a person? An animal or a human being? A beast or yourself? Do you understand? Do you hear me? (She slaps herself hysterically.) I'm talking to you, little baby! (In the voice of a child.) Mommy, mommy! (In her normal voice.) How many times do I have to tell you not to touch yourself there! Don't ever touch yourself again. It's bad to touch yourself, it's Satan!

Steps are heard. Someone is fumbling with a set of keys. The key turns in the lock, and turns and turns, as in a nightmare. Even the creaking of the hinges that accompanies the opening of the door goes on and on, maybe even too long, so that it grates (but it is necessarily so in the sense that every little event plays a psychological role, and is thus exaggerated). Enter Baphomet (alias the Stranger wearing a Devil mask).

STRANGER: Good evening!

LILA: You?

STRANGER: Unfortunately for you, but a bit for me too, I'm trapped inside the mechanism of your mind. I'd like it much better if I could get out, go for a walk, get some fresh air instead of having to breathe in the noxious atmosphere of this internal sewer. But I can't. I'm your prisoner.

LILA: No. I'm the one being held prisoner.
STRANGER: What can I tell you? I'm a creature of your own making, and that's all there is to it. That's the simple truth of the matter. Whether you like it or not.
LILA: Prove it.
STRANGER: You think about me and I exist. You stop thinking about me, and I vanish. It depends on you, Lila, on you, the life you make me embody. Despite myself. Satan exists, it's true, but inside o Man, who is his Creator. And you, well, you created me out of nothing: murderer! Look at me, look how ugly I am, repulsive. But you made me in your own image, monster that you are!

Lila sings her lullaby and covers her ears with her hands so she won't have to listen.

LILA: The swan of my imagining.
how black and ever darkening
it knows each pain and sorrow
that stirs within my marrow:
and I am left here all alone
so terrified of my dark zone.
STRANGER: It's time. Her descent into herself has ended with her

spirit coming to rest with a thud: her soul has reached its destination in the kingdom of darkness. Now, now! It's ready for the final leap into hell. There, unvanquished and unopposed, the bestial side of her humanity is galloping about, ready now, to inflict evil. (To her) Look in the mirror, Lila. Now you're really yourself, now I recognize you.

LILA No, I am not that monster!

STRANGER-BAPHOMET: There's no way out when you've damned yourself, when you've voluntarily locked yourself up in a mental hell. Maybe the disease we have to recover from is that of being human. We should be condemned at birth only for the fault of having been born! Blessed is the person who has never seen the light of day, who is not, who never has been and who never will be. He'll never have regrets, or shattered dreams, or an anxiety filled present. Nothing! An unattainable tranquillity and best of all, imperturbable. Within that nothingness there not even God or sin will be present; only inexhaustible time which has never been lived nor can ever be lived. Abstract, unknown, emptied. Understand? No? It doesn't matter, really. Let's go even deeper down into the darkness of your consciousness, Lila. We've almost touched bottom, there where the light of reason becomes lost in the glare of a black light, in the darkness of eternity. You're losing the spark which is you...(beguiling, his voice is heard ever further away as the lights dim.) Adieu, Lila, adieu...

(Black)

BAPHOMET'S LAST APPEARANCE (epilogue)

Baphomet, on hell's throne, reads from an ancient book, while Lila lies obscenely at his feet.

"Man, who considers himself God's masterpiece, could provide us with the proof of the incapacity or malice of the presumed Creator. In this sensitive, intelligent, thinking being who deems himself worthy of God's attention and who fashions God in his own image, we can only see a fragile machine which is defective and subject to malfunctions. Would it not be better, then, to be a machine without a soul rather than a superstitious and constantly anxious thing squirming under the yoke of his God and the thought of the infinite torments which await him in his future life?"

LILA: Miaaaow!

BAPHOMET Very good, Lila. Now you've understood everything! Spinoza my foot!

LILA: Miaaaow!

BAPHOMET: Bow wow! *They entwine themselves into one another and kiss.*

EIN UNGEHEUER NAMENS LILA
Deutsch von Sabyne Heymann

Sabyne Heymann über Enrico Bernard

Auf den allerersten Blick scheinen Bernards Texte harmloses Unterhaltungstheater mit leicht boulevardeskem Einschlag zu sein. Tatsächlich aber experimentiert der Autor mit allen erdenklichen Formen der Theatergeschichte. Manchmal beginnen seine Stücke wie eine Gesellschafts oder eine frenetische Situationskomödie, manchmal wie ein Konversationsstück, nur um unmittelbar darauf, sobald der Zuschauer sich in Sicherheit wähnt, ins Groteske umzukippen, von der Komödie zur Tragödie zu warden, vom Kabarett zum Zirkus. Die Kritiker haben seine Texte, die sich der Definition zu entziehen scheinen, irgendwo zwischen dem Futurismus und dem Theater des Absurden angesiedelt. Unter der Oberfläche der vermeindlichen "commedia brillante" verbirgt sich ein erschreckendes Szenarium des Unterbewussten, der alltäglichen Schizophrenie.

Bernards Stücke bewegen sich immer hart an den Abgründen der menschlichen Existenz: des Wahnsinns, des Bösen (als anthropologischer Konstante?). Er evoziert die Gespenster der Einsamkeit, oder einfach die Dummheit einer Welt, die dabei ist, vor aller Augen aus den Fugen zu greaten, in zusammenhanglose Fragmente zu zerfallen. Die Unfähigkeit der Menschen zur Kommunikation ist eines der zentralen Themen, über die Bernard mit dem klassischen Mittel des Theaters mit seinen Xuschauern in Kommunikation zu treten sucht. Obwehl sein Theater bestimmt nicht als klassisches Theater daherkommt, ist es dennoch eine sehr heutige Version der "Schaubühne als moralischer Anstalt"

Fest steht, daß bei Enrico Bernard nichts das ist, was es erscheint – und hier sind Berührungspunkte mit bester italienischer Pirandello-Tradition auszumachen. Schon über eines seiner frühen Stücke, "Da cosa nasce cosa" (deutsch etwa: "Eins ergibt sich aus dem andern") schrieb 1897 Renzo Tian, Grosskritiker der römischen Tageszeitung "Il Messaggero":

Die Leistung dieses Autors besteht darin, daß zwei oder drei Erzählebenen kunstvoll in ein Verhältnis zueinander gesetzt warden, sich gegenseitig bedingen, abstossen oder gar auslöschen. Durch ein subtiles Spiel von Montage und Demontage, den Einsatz eines kleinen, unkontrollierbaren Elements kann die normalste aller Situationen ganz plötzlich umkippen und eine völlig unvorhersehbare Wende nehmen, und schon schlittert die ganze Geschichte unaufhaltsam in dem Wahnsinn.

Bernard liebt es, in seinen Stücken an irgendeinem Punkt in unterschiedlischster Gestalt einen "Deus ex machina" einzusetzen, aber nicht etwa, um kurz vor der Katastrophe wundersam die unlösbare Verwicklung aufzulösen. Nein, sein "Deus ex machina" sorgt erst richtig für Verwirrung, bzw. Deckt sie auf und führt die Protagonisten in ein Labyrinth von Wiedersprüchen und Irrwegen, aus dem sie häufig nicht mehr herauskommen.

Gegen Ende der Achzigerjahre hat Enrico Bernard begonnen, seine Theorie eines "Teatro S-naturalista" zu entwickeln – ein kaum ins Deutsche übertragbarer Terminus: es handelt sich nämlich nicht einfach um ein "unnaturalistisches Theater", weil der Begriff im Italienischen auch das Wort "snaturato", also "entartet", mitschwingen lässt. Ent-naturalistisches Theater also? Jedenfalls will der Auto rein extrem nich-naturalistisches Theater.

Der Plot seines jüngsten Stückes "Ein Ungeheuer namens Lila" (Un mostro di nome Lila) soll hier nicht verraten warden, denn es hat, wie ein Thriller, zahlreiche überraschende Wendungen, lebt von Ambiguität und lässt verschiedene Interpretationsmöglichkeiten offen. Auch hier ist die Ausgangssituation scheinbar ganz normal: eine junge Frau, die einen abgelegenen, meist von Jäger besuchten Waldgasthof betreibt, erwacht im Morgengrauen. Sie hat einen Alptraum gehabt. Einen Alptraum? Oder sind die Ungeheuer ihres Traums nicht eigentlich fürchterlich real? Ist nicht tatsächlich ein "Ungeheuer" in der Gegend gesichtet worden? Wird sie von den Geistern ihres Unbewussten heimgesucht? Oder hat sie einfach eine schmutzige Phantasie? Verwirrt versucht sie, Tag und Traum voneinander zu unterscheiden, al sein "Unbekannter" den Gasthof betritt …

EIN UNGEHEUER NAMENS LILA

Personen:

Lila

Der Unbekannte

Incipit

Wer sich auf das Abenteuer dieses Stückes einlässt,
sollte sich nicht einbilden,
völlig ungeschoren wieder heauszukommen:
wenn ihr erst mal drin seid, last alle Hoffnung fahren!

Ganz plötzlich werdet ihr von einem entzetzlichen Schrei
überraschtm ja vernichtet warden.
Und ihr werdet euch fragen:
bin ich das, der da schreit, oder ist es irgendjemand,
der hinter mir her ist?

Doch, um in der Hölle zu landen,

braucht man in Wahrheit nur sich selbst zu erforschen:
wir alle, der eine mehr, der andere weniger,
sind verhinderte Ungeheuer.

Wer also wirklich vorhat, das Böse zu besiegen,
sollte dort mit dem Kampf beginnen,
wo es sich eingenistet hat:
in unserem eigenen Egoismus, nirgends sonst.
Denn es ist nicht denkbar, dass es das Werk
einer äusseren, anomalen, eben: monströsen! Gewalt ist,
wenn zu unserer Panik und zu unserem Entsetzen ein
Ungeheuer von uns Besitz ergriffen hat,
etwa eine aus dem Nichts entstandene Kraft, deren
Schicksal es wäre, nach einem trostlosen Erdenleben am
Rande der Normalität wieder dort zu verschwinden,
wo sie hergekommen ist.
Oh nein, meine Herrschaften, das Ungeheuer sind wir
selbst! Und es ist nicht einfach es zu vernichten,
weil wir den Mut aufbringen müssten,
einen chirurgischen Eingriff an uns selbst vorzunehmen.
Die Instinkte und der Blutdurst sind angeboren,
das beginnt schon mit der Durchtrennung der Nabelschnur
(und schmerzt mehr als der Tod!): damit wird der Dämon
des Lebens entfesselt, der sich unserer bemächtigt,
und nur mit Mühe, durch die Evolution des Gewissens,
durch Erziehung, durch Bildung kann man ihn
nicht immer, und nicht vollkommen) bändigen.
Doch es ist ein schwieriges Unterfangen,
ein langer Marsch durch dunkle Gefilde
voller Hindernisse und Fallen:
und wer den Weg ins Zentrum des Ichs,
zu unserem "Freund", dem Ungeheuer, verfehlt,
der läuft Gefahr, dasselbe Ende zu nehmen wie die
Protagonistin des Stückes, das Sie jetzt sehen warden.

Bühne:

Das Innere eines Berggasthofes an der deutsch-italienischen Sprachgrenze: es könnte sich um Südtirol oder das Tessin handeln. Die Geschichte spielt in der Gegenwart.
Es ist fünf Uhr morgens im eisigen Winter.
Draussen ist es noch dunkel, der Raum liegt im Halbschatten. Man hört den Wind und das Rauschen des Waldes. Die Schatten der Bäume, die sich schemenhaft durch ein

LILA Eine Nach war das! Kein Auge hab ich zugetan. Dieser Wind, es
schien ja fast, als ob er durch die Mauerritzen käme. Als ich dann diese
seltsamen, grauenhaften Stimmen hörte, hab ich angefangen zu zittern und
vor lauter Angst ist mir der kalte Schweiss ausgebrochen. Ich hab mich in
eine Ecke des Bettes zusammengerollt, in die Decke gewickelt und den
Kopf unter das Kissen gesteckt: ein höllisches Pfeifen mit Erscheinungen
von (schaudert es mich!) von zerstückelten Leichen, die sich zu Bergen
türmten. Das alles hat mir den Kopf so verwirrt, dass ich nicht einschlafen
konnte.

Leise singend, beim Kämmen:

Das Gespenst meiner bösen
Gedanken kennt die Qual,
Die mich im tiefsten bedrängt.
Wenn ich allein bleibe,
Habe ich Angst vor
Meiner dunklen Seite.

Ein Alptraum, wer   wess, warum! … Ich selbst bin auf mein Bett
zugegangenm in dem ich doch hilflos lag, als hätte ich mich verdoppelt, der
Hnker und sein Opfer. Von der Klinge des Messers, das ich hielt und in
mein anderes Ich hineingrubm ging ein bedrohliches Leuchten aus … Ich
kann die Worte, die ich dann aus meinem eigenen Munde vernahm, gar
nicht wiederholen! Aber das war gar nicht ich, die da sprach, das war ein
anderes Ich, mir völlig unbekannt und das … *(sie vergräbt das Gesicht in
den Händen)* Oh! Ein Glück, dass die Nacht vorbei ist, oder doch beinahe!
Im Sommer könnte man um die Zeit schon die Vögel singen hören …!
Statt dieser Dunkelheit, Larve eines Tages, der auf diese Weise von Beginn
an schon erloschen ist … *(erstaunt über ihre eigenen Worte)* Aber was sage ich

da, wie komme ich dazu, solche Worte zu sprechen. Ich bin doch nur ein einfaches, schüchternes Mädchen vom Lande ... und doch, wenigstens solange es Nacht ist, rede ich wie ein von Dämonen beflügelter Dichter ... Dämonen? Ein Dämon also ist es, der mit mir, durch mich, in mir spricht: wie ein Satz, der von leiser Stimme souffliert, nur wiederholt wird, ja, genau wie der Wind! Es ist der Dämon, der auch das Geäst der Pinien, die trockenen, gefrorenen Zweige der Eichen zum Rascheln bringt, damit die Bäume Namen, Dinge, Gedanken aussprechen, die jemand in mir ausstreut, wie Sperma verspritzt ... Was habe ich gesagt! Mein Gott, was habe ich gesagt? ... *(sie schlägt ein Kreuz)* Mein Geist streift in der Finsternis umher wie ein Blinder im Sonnenlicht. Schrecklich diese Einbildungen, die die Dämmerung hervorruft, die wirklichen Dinge verschwimmen und nehmen völlig neue Konturen an: der Schatten einer Stuhllehne verwandelt sich so in das teuflische Gelächter des Tisches, und die Lampe, die im Luftzug pendelt, wird zu der Fledermaus, in die Er sich verwandelt, der Herr der Finsternis in uns, einer Finsternis, die Er mit gespenstischem Schein erleuchtet: Luzifer, ja, das ist sein Name. Oder: der das Licht bringt, aber was für ein Licht!

Die Last meiner bösen
Gedanken kennt die Qual,
Die mic him tiefsten bedrängt.
Wenn ich allein bleibe,
Habe ich Angst vor
Meiner dunklen Seite.

Brav, Lila, sei brav. Schliesslich ist es nicht deine Schuld, wenn es nicht Sommer ist und wenn der pralle Phallus des Tages nocht nicht herausgekommen ist ... Warum sage ich "Phallus"? Was rede ich nur? Sataans Worte vielleicht ... Still, sei still, Mund! Sag nichts, was du nicht verstehst, was du nicht wissen kannst. Und wenn ich dir sage, dass du es nicht wissen kannst, must du mir glauben! *(Pause)* Gut, brav, Lila, jetzt sei ruhig und denk dran, dass das Fenster sich bald mit Licht benetzen wird. Das Licht wird sic him Zimnmer ausbreiten und in deinen Augen und in dein Hirn eindringen und es befrutchten ... Das Licht? Sein Licht will vielleicht in mich eindringen und mich befruchten: Luzifers Licht! Und ich kann ihm noch nicht einmal sagen: zurück!, weil ich von mir selbst besessen bin weil ich selbst mich ihm geöffnet habe, dem Saukerl, dem Schwein, mich mit seinen Eskrementen besudelt habe, mit seinem Urin und dem stinkenden Speichel, den er auf meinen Brustwarzen und Lippen zurückgelassen hat ... überall, wie ein Erinnerungszeichen, eine teuflische Mahnung, die besagt: du bist Fleisch! Doch das Fleisch, Lila, verwelkt, und

der Vater weiss, dass du gesündigt hast: er hat es gesehen, er hat es gehört
…

Schluss, Lila, jetzt reicht's. Du hast schon zu lange mit seiner Stimme
gesprochen, zuviele schlimme Worte sind aus deinen feuchten Lippen
gedrungen. Ein Lächeln zeichnet sich auf ihnen ab, umrahmt von dem
Lippenstift, mit dem du dich als Frau maskiert hast … *(verzweifelt)* Mama,
warum schlägst du mich? *(Mit erwachsener Stimme)* Du hast meinen
Lippenstift kaputtgemacht, da, der ist nicht mehr zu gebrauchen! In deinem
Alter spielst du schon die kleine Hure? *(Wird wieder zum Kind)* Und er, statt
mich zu trösten und auf starken Armen wegzutragen, straft mich und sagt,
dass es böse ist, böse!, dass ich Frau und Kind bin! Hässlich! Böse! *(weint)*
Hör auf zu weinen, du bist jetzt gross und nu rim Traum kannst du es dir
noch erlauben, wieder die zu warden die du mal warst. Und Träume sind ja
so unwirklich, es lohnt sich gar nicht, darüber nachzudenken! Wem nützt
das schon? Tja, vielleicht uns selbst: um uns wehzutun oder dem Bösen,
das wir in uns haben und das irgendwie ja raus muss … aber was versteh
ich schon von Träumen! Ich jammere hier herum, und dabei muss noch
das Lokal in Ordnung gebracht warden bevor aufgemacht wird … (kehrt
noch einmal zu ihrem verherigen Gedankengang zurück) Die Träume sind
doch nur ein Ort der Ungewissheit, wo die Vernunft eine leere Hülse ist,
wie ein Totenschädel … Ach!, was mir nur im Kopf herungeht! Halt ein,
due verrückter Kopf, bevor es zu spat ist ich habe geträumt, dass ich von
Papa einen giftigen Pilz bekommen habe … *(kommt wieder zu sich)* Die
Hörnchen sind noch nicht geliefert worden, ich werde einfach die von
gestern nochmal aufwärmer, verschlafen, wie sie sind, warden sie es gar
nicht merken … Ich habe wirklich etwas komisches geträumt, ich kann es
mir nicht erklären: es war, als ob die Dinge keine Dichte mehr hätten, als
ob ich um sie herumfliessen würde: sie boten meinem Körper keinen
Widerstand, er war also nicht vorhanden. Substanzlos sank ich in sie ein.
Selbst mein Bettzeug schien wie eine Welle, die mich überschwemmte und
meinen Atem, mein Dasein im Nichts erstickte: ein immenser mentales
Ozean tobte in mir und zog mich in einen Strudel ohne Ende. Und, am
Fusse jenes Abgrunds riss ein Ungeheuer seine Feueraugen auf … Ach, wie
entsetzlich! *(verbirgt den Kops in ihren Händen)*

*Hinter Lilas Rücken, von ihr zunächst unbemerkt, erscheint, leicht hinkend, der
Unbekannte. Er trägt einen anonymen Übergangsmantel und einen schwarzen Hut mit
breiter Krempe. Er trägt einen Koffer bei sich.*

UNBEKANNTER Gewisse üble Träume sollte man lieber den
Ungeheuern überlassen, mein Fräulein.
LILA *(überrascht)* Wer … wer sind Sie denn?

UNBEKANNTER Eigentlich möchte ich nur frühstücken, wenn es recht ist.

LILA Ich habe gar nicht gehört, wie Sie hereingekommen sind.

UNBEKANNTER Ja, das hab ich gemerkt. Ich bin extra leise hereingekommen. Weil ich Ihr, wie sol lich es nennen?, ja: Ihr Selbstgespräch nicht unterbrechen wollte.

LILA Sie können es ruhig sagen: mein Gefasel.

UNBEKANNTER Jetzt übertreiben Sie. Allenfalls war es ein harmloser innerer Monolog. Jedenfalls brauchen Sie nichts zu befürchten: da war weder etwas Beunruhigendes, noch etwas Kompromittierendes. Das können Sie mir glauben! Allenfalls ein passegerer Alterationszustand aufgrund, was Weiss ich?, des Vollmonds. Oder eine flüchtige Überreiztheit, hervorgerufen durch die milde Wärme der Bettdecke. Sowas kann das Hirn schon dazu verleiten, den Körper für eine unartikulierte, einzig vom LP beherrschte Einheit zu halten, jenem Urinstinkt des Menschen, den man "Lustprinzip" nennt.

LILA Ich verstehen nicht ganz, aber … träme ich? *(Unsicher)* Sie sind wirklich, nicht wahr? Ich meine: Sie sind fast durchsichtig, wie lichdurchflutet, von einem seltsamen Licht … einem Licht, das es auf der Erdoberfläche eigentlich nicht gibt …

UNBEKANNTER Duchsichtig, ich? Kann sein: ich habe seit gestern Abend nichts mehr gegessen und heute morgen habe ich noch nicht gefrühstückt.

LILA Aber, verzeihen Sie, wenn ich noch einmal darauf zurückkomme, Sie scheinen wirklich aus Luft zu bestehen … als ob Sie einem dieser Luftwirbel entsprungen seien, die durch die Fensterritzen dringen. Sind Sie ganz sicher, dass Sie nicht … ?

UNBEKANNTER Na, das ist ja fein! Sie halten mich wohl für einen Gest? Nein, es tut mir leid, Sie enttäuschen zu müssen. Ich bin nicht Ihrem Traum entstiegen, beziehungsweise: Alptraum (Sie scheinen der Typ zu sein, der sogar mit offenen Augen träumt). Jedenfalls, dieses "Ungeheuer", das Sie am Abgrund Ihres Strudels haben auftauchen sehen, das bin ich nicht … so war es doch? Nein, nein, schauen Sie, ich sag es noch einmal: ich bin nur ein Gast. Vielleicht der erste zu dieser Stunde, aber irgendjemand muss ja der erste sein. Also, ich oder jemand anders … Oder habt ihr noch zu?

LILA Um die Zeit machen wir auf.

UNBEKANNTER Das ist keine ernsthafte Antwort. Ist das Lokal offen oder geschlossen? Sagen Sie es klar heaus, sonst gehe ich wieder.

LILA Ich muss mich nur fertig frisieren, dann bediene ich Sie sofort.

UNBEKANNTER Ich muss leider weiter. Ausserdem glaube ich, dass ich mich verfähren habe. Deshalb bin ich an diesen einsamen Ort greaten.

Als die Strasse zu Ende war, wo der Wald beginnt, da habe ich mir gesagt: zum Teufel auch, du endest noch wie der grosse Meister Dante … von wegen dem "dunklen Wald", verstehen Sie? Ich bin da eine Weile heumgeirrt und habe dann gesehen, dass in diesem Gasthof das Licht an war. So habe ich angehalten und mir gesagt: das ist ein Jagdgebiet, vielleicht Machen die schon auf, habe ich mir gesagt und bin ausgestiegen.

LILA Und was haben Sie sich gesagt, nachdem Sie ausgestiegen waren?

UNBEKANNTER Hab verstanden, Sie machen sich lustig über mich. Ich kann's verstehen, wenn man sich auch so blöd verirrt … ich bin von der Autobahn runtergefahren, weil dieses dauernde Geradeausfahren mich ganz verrückt gemacht hat … wissen Sie, ich bin die ganze Nacht durchgefahren. So hab ich auf die Schnellstrasse gewechselt, um mich mit den Kurven ein bisschen wachzuhalten. Dann kam diese Landstrasse, die Serpentinen, bis ich auf diesem Maultierpfad gelandet bin …

LILA Sie haben Glück: er ist erst vor kurzem asphaltiert worden. Eigentlich sollte der Wald gerodet warden, um einen Zubringer zur Autobahn zu bauen. Aber da haben sich die Umweltschützer ins Zeug gelegt, und es ist nichts draus geworden. Schade, für das Dorf wär es ein Geschäft geworden.

UNBEKANNTER Ja, dann hätte ich statt des Waldfasthofes ein Autobahnrestaurant mit 24 Stunden Self Service vorgefunden.

LILA Und ein warmes Buffett.

UNBEKANNTER Für die Ferbfahrer.

LILA Die sind immer noch besser als die Jäger. Die halten sich nämlich für was höheres, nur weil sie ein Gewehr haben …

UNBEKANNTER Ihr Hass auf die Gewehre bedeutet, dass Sie den Elektrakomplex noch nicht völlig überwunden haben, oder dass Sie, wie der grosse Siegmund behaupten würde, noch Penisneid empfinden.

LILA Ich verstehen Sie nicht. Ich Weiss nicht, wer dieser Siegmund sein soll. Sie sind ziemlich arrogant emir gegenüberm wenn ich das mal sagen darf. Sie nehmen sich ganz schöne Freiheiten heraus, nur weil Sie wissen, dass ich mich nicht traue, Ihnen so zu antworten, wie Sie es verdient hätten. Seien Sie also so freundlich und hören Sie auf, mich mit Ihren Zweideutigkeiten zu belästigen. Ich Weiss sowieso, worauf ihr immer hinauswollt.

UNBEKANNTER Nun mal langsam: Ihre sexuellen Frustrationen sind mir, ehrlich gesagt, ziemlich egal. Ich hätte nur gern einen Kaffee und dann möchte ich, dass Sie mir zeigen, wie ich hier wieder rauskomme … aber ja, nennen wir es ruhig beim Namen, wie ich aus diesem *finstern Wald*, aus diesem *Infermo dantesco* wieder herauskomme.

LILA Auf den Kaffee müssen Sie noch einen Augenblick warten. Ich muss erst die Espressomaschine anmachen.

UNBEKANNTER *(resigniert)* Dann werde ich eben warten!

LILA Warum setzen Sie sich nicht?

UNBEKANNTER Sie Machen wohl Witze? Ich habe die ganze Nacht im Auto gesessen! Ich will mir ein bisschen die Beine vertreten, wie soll ich sonst noch mal tausend Kilometer fahren.

LILA Wo wollen Sie denn hin? Ans Ende der Welt?

UNBEKANNTER Warum nicht? Im Grunde genommen ist die Welt doch gar nicht so gross.

LILA Wollen Sie in den Süden?

UNBEKANNTER Ja, in die Hölle, wenn Sie erlauben.

LILA Nehmen Sie es mir doch nicht übel. Wir sind hier nun einmal so. Das Dorf ist klein, alle kennen sich untereinander, keener hat Geheimnisse … Sie sind natürlich völlig frei, hinzufahren, wo Sie wollen, auch in den Süden. Dort wird es auch ansäbdige Leute geben wie Sind und ich. Verzeih'n Si emir?

UNBEKANNTER Schon gut, es tut mir leid! Die Müdigkeit bringt mich dazu, Dinge zu sagen, die eigentlich nicht meine Art sind, im Gegenteil …

LILA Nein, ich bin zu weit gegangen … es ist ohnehin an der Zeit, mit dieser Nord-Südgeschichte aufzuhören, als ob es nicht auch Ost-West gäbe. *(Wechselt den Tonfall)* Wissen Sie, ich habe auch eine aufregende Nacht hinter mir… aber, ist es eigentlich noch Nacht?

UNBEKANNTER Weder Nacht, noch Tag, diese Grauzone in der die Geschöpfe der Finsternis – die Traumgestalten – ganz schnell wieder an ihre Ursprungsorte zurückkehren, solange tas Tageslicht die Dunkelheit noch nicht völlig aufgelöst hat.

LILA Sie reden so kompliziert … und dennoch verstehen ich, ode rich glaube zu verstehen … seltsam!

UNBEKANNTER Darüber wundern Sie sich?

LILA Sollte ich nicht?

UNBEKANNTER Es wird immer gesagt, dass dies die Stunde der armen Seelen ist.

LILA Meiner zum Beispiel.

UNBEKANNTER Das sind die, die noch nicht zur Hölle herabgestiegen sind, aber auch den Weg ins Paradies nicht gefaunden haben. Es ist eine Art Fegefeuer, in dem Ungeheuer herumspucken, die zu feige sind, ihre Grausamlkeit voll auszuleben: es sind unvollkommene, unfertige Monster ohne Sinn und Zweck, Ausgeburten inkonsequenter Phantasien, Hirngespinste, Strohfeuer, die sich entzünden, um sich selbst zu wärmen an ihrer theatralischen Abstraktion, ihrer tragischen, aber – mit Verlaub – ein wenig onanistischen Isolation! Masturbation des Geistes, der sich von den Sonnenstrahlen leuchten lässt. Wozu also die eigenen monströsen Gedanken in dieses Fegefeuer treiben lassen, in dem alles nur Rauch ist, Erscheinung ohne Inhalt?

LILA Verzeih'n Sie, aber ich k ann Ihnen, glaube ich, nicht folgen.

UNBEKANNTER Ich habe gesagt: warum, warum soll man an das Ungeheuer, das in uns ist, nur abstract denken, statt …

LILA Weiss ich nicht, ich will es auch gar nicht wissen.

UNBEKANNTER Oder haben Sie Angst, es laut auszusprechen?

LILA Und wenn schon?

UNBEKANNTER Was ist den schon dabei! Machen Sie sich frei davon!

LILA Ich habe Angst, ganz allgemein. Genau wie sie eben gesagt haben: eine abstrakte Angst.

UNBEKANNTER *(versucht, sie zu beruhigen)* Sie warden sehen, dass beim ersten Morgenrot Ihre angeborenen (und ein wenig kindischen, tut mir leid) Ängste sich in Luft auflösen: und im klaren Kelch des Lebens *(verzeihen Sie diese Emphase, aber wenn schon, den schon)* wird kein Blut mehr fliessen, sondern ein grüner Saft, vital wie die Blätter und Keime im Frühling. Zufrieden?

LILA Aus dem Weg, husch! Sehen Sie nicht, dass ich arbeite?

UNBEKANNTER Sie machen einen groben Fehler, wenn Sie blind dem Tag vertrauen, der gerade erwacht. Aber, wenn Sie erlauben, noch ist er ja nicht da. Eine Sonne, die noch nicht aufgegangen ist, das ist in etwa so wie Bankzinsen, die noch nicht fällig sind.

LILA Im Reden sind Sie stark!!

UNBEKANNTER Es stimmt aber. Der Tag begünstigt den klaren, rationalen Gedanken, während die Dunkelheit das Hirn vernebelt; ist ein bisschen peinlich. *(Pause)* Sie haben schöne Beine, wissen Sie das?

LILA Ich? Krumm sind sie.

UNBEKANNTER Amazonenbeine. Reiten Sie?

LILA Ich reite schon, ader nur auf dem Motorrad.

UNBEKANNTER Sie sind also sportlich.

LILA Wenn mich diese peinlichen Phantasien verfolgen, dann setze ich den Helm auf und fahr los, ganz ohne Ziel, ich fahr einfach herum, manchmal sogar im Kreis, wie eine Blöde. Es ist ja nicht das erste Mal, dass …

UNBEKANNTER Was den für Phantasien? Sexuelle, oder was?

LILA *(ärgerlich)* Also, entschuldigen Sie mal!

UNBEKANNTER Sie sind völlig frei, die Auskunft zu verweigern, um Himmels Willen!

LILA Das fehlte auch noch …

UNBEKANNTER Wenn ich sie wäre, würde ich aber darüber reden.

LILA Und weshalb?

UNBEKANNTER Zuviel Druck, die Maschine knallt gleich durch.

LILA Wie kommen Sie den darauf, dass ich unter Druck stehe, he?

UNBEKANNTER Das sieht man.

LILA Ach, tacsächlich? Und woran sieht man das?

UNBEKANNTER Der Dampf. Ja, sehen Sie den nicht, dass gleich die Espressomasschine in die Luft fliegt, hinter Ihnen. Ich sehe es aber. Los, machen Sie schnell, bevor sie explodiert. Verdammt nochmal, hören Sie den nicht, gleich fliegt sie in die Luft! Tun Sie was!

In der Tata sieht man hinter der Theke eine dichte Dampfwolke aufsteigen.

LILA Ja, doch … *(wütend, zur Kaffeemaschine, während sie sich an ihr zu schaffen macht)* Strega!

UNBEKANNTER Frauen und Technik, Freude und Schmerz!

LILA Reden Sie nicht so'n Quatsch!

UNBEKANNTER Ich versuche nur, mich auf andere Gedanken zu bringen: ich habe nämlich einen Bärenhunger, und wenn ich nicht sofort einen Kaffee kriege, fange ich an zu brummen. Wollen Sie's hören? Hier: Hhhmmm!

LILA Leider müssen Sie sich noch ein bisschen gedulden, Herr Brummbär! *(Murmelt)* Das klingt richtig echt!

UNBEKANNTER Noch mehr! Also, das grenzt schon an Folter!

LILA Ich hab die Maschine erst mal leergemacht, manchmal klemmt nämlich das Ventil und die Luft geht nicht durch. Jetzt müsste sie wieder unter Druck stehen … haben Sie noch einen kleinen Moment Geduld.

UNBEKANNTER Der Gast wird zur Geduld angehalten. Netter Service! Bedienung inbegriffen!

LILA In der Zwischenzeit werde ich die Frühstückstische decken. Wollen Sie mir inicht helfen, statt hier im Weg zu stehen?

UNBEKANNTER Auch das noch, kommt ja überhaupt nicht in Frage!

LILA Faulpelz!

UNBEKANNTER Wieso sollte ich Ihnen beim Tischdecken helfen?

LILA Da würde ich Zeit gewinnen.

UNBEKANNTER Und was gewinne ich, wenn ich Ihnen helfe?

LILA Ihren Kaffee. Wollen Sie sonst irgendwas? Ein Hörnchen vielleicht?

UNBEKANNTER Sie sind zu gütig.

LILA Schon gut! Sowie der Bäcker kommt, spendier ich Ihnen ein Hörnchen.

UNBEKANNTER Und wenn er nicht kommt?

LILA Warum sollte er den nicht kommen?

UNBEKANNTER Wegen der Panik … Das Ungeheuer, Sie wissen doch.

LILA Was für ein Ungeheuer? Was meinen Sie damit?

UNBEKANNTER Tun Sie doch nicht so, ich bin schliesslich nicht von gestern.

LILA *(misstrauisch)* Sie sind doch nur auf der Durchreise. Wie können Sie dann wissen, was bei uns los ist?

UNBEKANNTER Ich lese schliesslich Zeitung, über den Fall ist doch überall berichtet worden. Sie … Sie lessen wohl nicht?

LILA *(ausweichend)* Doch, doch … wenn ich Zeit habe.

UNBEKANNTER Und … Radio hören Sie auch?

LILA Wenn ich Zeit habe.

UNBEKANNTER Und … gucken Sie Fernsehen?

LILA *(ärgerlich)* Wenn ich Zeit habe?

UNBEKANNTER Wann haben Sie den Zeit?

LILA Wenn man mich in Ruhe die Tische decken lässt, da Si emir ja anscheinend nicht helfen wollen.

UNBEKANNTER Wenn ed Ihnen Freude macht …

LILA Ich wette, es ist das erste Mal, dass Sie irgendeine Hausarbeit verrichten.

UNBEKANNTER Das erste und Letzte Mal.

LILA Und was sagt Ihre Frau dazu? *(sie überreicht ihm ein Tablett mit Geschirr).*

UNBEKANNTER Ich bin nicht verheiratet.

LILA Sie warden doch eine Freundin haben, irgendein Mädchen …

UNBEKANNTER Nein, nein: besser allein als in schlechter Gesellschaft.

LILA Es ist besser, ich rede überhaupt nicht mit Ihnen. Ich ärgere mich sowieso nur.

Gemeinsam machen sie sich daren, die Tische zu decken.
Lila trällert ihr Liedchen, während der Unbekannte sie betrachtet, als würde er irgendetwas aushecken.

LILA Der Schrein meiner bösen
Gedanken kennt die Qual,
die mich im tiefsten bedrängt.
Wenn ich allein bleibe,
Habe ich Angst
Vor dem Dunkel in mir.

UNBEKANNTER Gut! Sie singen wie ein Engelchen.

LILA Ich bin kein Engel.

UNBEKANNTER *(ironisch)* Ein Ungeheuer aber auch nicht.

LILA Wer weiss …

UNBEKANNTER *(im Scherz)* Da hab ich aber Angst! *(Kurz darauf)* Haben Sie eigentlich keine Ankst vor dem Ungeheuer?

LILA Ich? Weshalb sollte ich? Ich habe nie jemandem etwas Böses zugefügt!

UNBEKANNTER Gut, aber auf solche Feinheiten achtet ein Ungeheuer doch nicht ... ein hübsches Fohlen wie Sie, ganz allein ... Sie schmeissen den Laden hier doch allein, nich wahr?

LILA Keine Fragen, hatten wir abgemacht.

UNBEKANNTER Wann hätten wir das denn abgemacht?

LILA Ahh! Ich dachte, ich hätte so etwas gehört ... *(als ob ihr plötzlih ein Licht aufgeht)* Deswegen sind die Jäger seit ein paar Tagen wie vom Erdboden verschluckt.

UNBEKANNTER Die sind wohl alle auf der Jagd nach dem Ungeheuer?

LILA Ach was! Die scheissen sich doch vor lauter Angst in die Hosen ... Die sind doch nur mutig, wenn sie irgendwelche armen Lerchen schiessen und warden zu wahren Helde, wenn sie den Mädchen an die Wäsche gehen. Aber wenn es um ein Ungeheuer geht, ziehen sie alle den Schwanz ein und laufen nach Hause zur Mami, die wartet schon mit dem Nudelholz. Und sowas nennt sich Männer! Die haben sich genauso dünngemacht wie ihre Vögelchen! *(lacht frech)*

UNBEKANNTER Ich hab mich aber nicht dünngemacht, weder ich, noch mein Vögelchen, ich bin hier ... *(sie blickt ihn finster an)* Da vergeht Ihnen wohl das Lachen? Habe ich irgendetwas unpassendes gesagt? War die Anspieleung vielleicht ein bisschen zu deutlich?

LILA Sie sind nicht von hier. Sie sind auf der Durchreise. Wieso sollte es das Ungeheuer ausgerechnet auf Sie abgesehen haben?

UNBEKANNTER Wenn es ein Ungeheuer ist, nehme ich mal an, dass es verrückt ist. Oder nicht? Und bei den Verrückten, meine Liebe, ist mit Logik nicht viel auszurichten.

LILA Selbst wenn es verrückt ist, irgendeine verrückte Logik wird es doch haben ...

UNBEKANNTER Was Sie alles zu wissen glauben!

LILA Weibliche Intuition.

UNBEKANNTER Das heist, Sie nehmen es in Schutz.

LILA Wer, ich? Nein, wie kommen Sie den darauf? Ich meine nur, dass Verrückte nicht immer Ungeheuer sind, manchmal sind sie auch grosse Künstler, wie Cezanne oder dieser andere, dieser berühmte, der sich das Oher abgeschnitten hat.

UNBEKANNTER Alles, was mit Künstlern zu tun hat, hängt irgendwie auch mit dem Wahnsinn zusammen, obwohl man die Kunst nich für das Vorrecht einiger weniger Wahnsinniger halten sollte, die sich zur Avantgarde der geistigen Katastrophe des Menschen auserkoren fühlen.

LILA Dazu kann ich nichts sagen. Sonst wäre ich auch nicht in der Lage, den Tisch zu decken … Scusi! Entschuldigung … also, wir sollten wohl besser das Thema wechseln.

UNBEKANNTER Gut, aber bitte keine Politik. Politik finde ich zum Kotzen.

LILA Ich auch. Einverstanden: weder Ungeheuer, noch Politiker.

UNBEKANNTER Reden wir doch über uns, über unsere Angelegenheiten, in dieser Stunde der Intimität vor Tagesanbruch.

LILA Jetzt bilden Sie sich bloss nichts ein.

UNBEKANNTER *(stell sich ahnungslos)* Wer? Ich?

LILA Ja, genau Sie: was wollen Sie den mit Ihren plumpen Andeutungen erreichen?

UNBEKANNTER Gar nichts, ich schwör's. *(Ironisch)* Ich bin eine ernsthafte Person.

LILA Hören Sie: Sie sind für miche in x-beliebiger Gast, der hier seinen Kaffee trinkt.

UNBEKANNTER Den hab ich aber immer noch nicht bekommen. Und ausserdem werde ich hier unter Strafandrohung ausgebeutet: arbeite, Sklave!, keine Widerrede … sehen Sie mal, ich hab schon zwei Tische fertig: Sie warden doch sicher beim Chef ein gutes Wort für mich einlegen, damit er mich einstellt, nicht?

LILA Ich bin hier die Chefin.

UNBEKANNTER Aha! Dann ist das Ihr Gasthaus … na schön! Eine gute Partie!

LILA Von meiner Familie lebt keiner mehr, ich habe weder Verwandte, noch Freunde. Ich bin ganz allein auf der Welt. Und mir geht's gut dabei. Nur nachts krieg ich's manchmal ein bisschen mit der Angst, aber ansonsten komme ich ausgezeichnet zurecht. Sogar mit der Steuererklärung. Ich brauche niemanden, noch nicht mal einen Steuerberater.

UNBEKANNTER Sie sind sehr tüchtig, wirklich. Aber … verzeihen Sie mcinc Ncugierde, Sie sind noch so jung … Ihre Familie? Sind Sie Waise? Ein Unglück?

LILA Interessiert Sie das?

UNBEKANNTER Lassen Sie mich raten, ich bitte Sie: einer von diesen dummen Verkehrsunfällen, vermutlich wegen erhöhter Geschwindigkeit, vielleicht auch noch zuwenig Luft in den Reifen. Hab ich Recht?

LILA Woher wissen Sie das?

UNBEKANNTER Ich hab greaten, mit Hilfe der Statistik Verkehrsunfälle sind heute tatsächlich die häufigste Todesursache – und ich habe ins Schwarze getroffen.

LILA *(ironisch)* Bravo!

UNBEKANNTER Wieso war eigentlich so wenig Luft in den Reifen? Bestimmt nicht us Nachlässigkeit des lieben Verstorbenen: es stimmt doch, dass Ihr Vater äusserst penibel war und bei jedem Tanken del Luftdruck prüfen liess?

LILA Hören Sie auf! Sie stecken Ihre Nase dauernd in Dinge, die Sie nichts angehen!

UNBEKANNTER Und Ihre Adoptiveltern, die sich so sehr ein kleines Mädchen gewünscht hatten, aber selbst keine Kinder haben konnten – und hier kommt Ihr Auftritt, mit blonden Zöpfen, versteht sich! – sind die nicht auch durch tragische Umstände ums Leben gekommen? Eine undichte Gasleitung?

LILA Tragische Umstände, genau.

UNBEKANNTER Und Ihr Verlobter, ist er nicht bei einem Bergunfall umgekommen, und zwar einen Tag, nachdem er Sie entjungfert hatte. Ist der wirklich abgestürzt?

LILA *(aufbrausend)* Was wollen Sie von mir?

UNBEKANNTER Nichts, gar nichts. Sie brauchen sich nicht aufzuregen. Ich will damit nur sagen, dass Sie ganz einfach Pech gehabt haben, sehr viel Pech, vielleicht ein bisschen zu viel; aber dass Sie trotz des Unglücks, von dem Sie verfolgt werden, und obwohl Sie so entsetzliche Schicksalsschläge abgekriegt haben, sich wieder hochgerappelt haben, sich hier gans allein durchschlagen. Wir haben es heute sogar mit einem echten Profi zu tun, einer richtigen Unternehmerin, einem Genie der Marktwirtschaft! Tüchtig!

LILA Wir, wer wir?

UNBEKANNTER Pluralis majestatis.

LILA Na gut, Ihre Majestät mögen siche bequemen, ich mach jetzt Kaffee.

UNBEKANNTER Na, das wird aber auch Zeit! Und die Croissants?

LILA Eins nach dem anderen, ich bitte Sie!

(Schickt sich an, zur Theke zu gehen, stolpert aber über den Koffer).

UNBEKANNTER Vorsicht!

LILA Merda! Jetzt hätte ich mir beinahe den Hals gebrochen. Wie sind Sie nur auf die Idee gekommen, den Koffer hier abzustellen. Ich bring ihn in die Garderobe, hier steht er im Weg … *(will ihn nehmen)*

UNBEKANNTER *(mit einer nervösen Bewegung)* Rühren Sie ihn nich an!

LILA Mein Gott, ist der schwer.

UNBEKANNTER Bitte gehen Sie vorsichtig damit um … sachte …

LILA Ich fass ihn ja gar nicht an … schaffen Sie ihn doch selbst weg, wenn Sie dazu in der Lage sind.

UNBEKANNTER *(stellt den Koffer unter den Tisch)* So, jetzt steht er nicht mehr im Weg.

LILA Sind da Steine drin? Der wiegt mindstens einen Zentner.

UNBEKANNTER Genau, Steine. Wie haben Sie das erraten?

LILA Wollen Sie mich auf den Arm nehmen?

UNBEKANNTER Sie haben mit den Steinen angefangen.

LILA Ja, aber nicht im Ernst.

UNBEKANNTER Wenn ich Ihnen jetzt erzählen würde, dass ich ein Geologe bin und in diesem Koffer eine Sammlung von Felsproben habe, würden Sie mir das abnehmen?

LILA Nein.

UNBEKANNTER *(lachend)* Da täten Sie auch gut dran. Nein, Steine sind da nicht drin!

LILA Was denn sonst?

UNBEKANNTER Gallium. Wissen Sie, was das ist?

LILA Nee! Ich kenn nur die Gallier.

UNBEKANNTER Gallium ist eine neue Metallegierung. Aud den Militärlabors der ehemaligen Sowjetunion. Gallium ist ein Superstromleiter, glaube ich.

LILA Und jemand, der so etwas gefährliches, geheimnisvolles transportiert, der verirrt sich hierher in dieses von Gott und dem Teufel verlassene Bergnest?

UNBEKANNTER Vom Teufel ja nun bestimmt nicht. Der vergisst nie jemanden oder etwas.

LILA Wissen Sie eigentlich, dass Sie ein komischer Typ sind?

UNBEKANNTER Wirklich? Hab ich ein Ohrfeigengesicht?

LILA Um diese Zeit, in der Dämmerung, sind Sie eine ziemlich ungewöhnliche Erscheinung, das können Sie nicht leugnen, ich habe jemanden wie Sie hier in der Gegend noch nie gesehen, Sie werden doch nicht etwa …

UNBEKANNTER Das Ungeheuer? Warum nicht? *(lacht)*

LILA Sie brauchen nicht gleich beleidigt zu sein … hm!

UNBEKANNTER Um Gottes Willen! Ich bin nicht der Typ, der gleich einschnappt, im Gegenteil …

LILA Im Gegenteil, es gefällt Ihnen sogar.

UNBEKANNTER Genau! Aber ich würde gern von Ihnen hören, was Sie von mir halten, ganz unvoreingenommen: wer bin ich?

LILA Woher soll ich das wissen?

UNBEKANNTER Ein Ungeheuer, na gut. Aber das wäre zu einfach.

LILA Wieso denn?

UNBEKANNTER Weil doch alle Fremden, wohl oder über, ein bisschen seltsam wirken. Und ein Ungeheuer ist doch etwas, was nicht in die Norm passt, eben seltsam wirkt, nicht wahr? Ein bisschen finster, merkwürdig, oder, wenn wir es ganz klar ausdrücken wollen, abstossend.

Ist das nicht genau der Eindruck, den ich, ohne mein Zutun, auf Sie mache?

LILA Ich weiss nicht.

UNBEKANNTER Los, reden Sie. Ganz offen. Ich bin nicht nachtragend, mich interessiert nur Ihre unvoreingenommene Meinung, auch wenn sie vielleicht ein bisschen oberflächlich ist!

LILA Ich sag es Ihnen noch einmal: ich weiss es nicht. Ich kenne Sie viel zu wenig.

UNBEKANNTER Wozu müssen Sie mich kennen? Sehen Sie mich nicht? Hören Sie mich nicht?

LILA *(ärgerlich)* Aber was reden Sie da?

UNBEKANNTER *(zweideutig)* Nichts, gar nichts …

LILA Na, endlich.

UNBEKANNTER Oder alles.

LILA Fangen Sie schon wieder an?

UNBEKANNTER Ich würde wirklich gern wissen, was Sie von mir halten … Geben Sie sich doch mal ein bisschen Mühe!

LILA Na gut, wenn Sie unbedingt wollen: von Ihren Augen geht eine seltsame Ausstrahlung aus, sie sind wie entzündet.

UNBEKANNTER Meine Augen, entzündet? Sind Sie sicher?

LILA Ja: sie ziehen mich an und gleichzeitig stossen sie mich ab, wie ein Leuchtturm, der die Nähe eines Hafens anzeigt, aber auch ein gefährliches Riff.

UNBEKANNTER Hört, hört: wie ein Dichter reden wir plötzlich daher! In Bildern! In Metaphern sogar!

LILA Hören Sie, ich kann mich nicht besser ausdrücken.

UNBEKANNTER Ich kann Ihnen gern ein paar Worte leihen, wenn Sie wollen, das habe ich bisher ja auch getan.

LILA Sie …? Dass ich nicht lache.

UNBEKANNTER Lachen Sie nur.

LILA Sie sind verrückt!

UNBEKANNTER Ja, vollkommen. Aber Sie sind nicht aufrichtig.

LILA Was wollen Sie noch wissen?

UNBEKANNTER Du hast wohl keine Lust, mir dein Herz ganz zu öffnen, du miese kleine Hure!?

Er packt ihren Arm und drückt ihn, dass er wehtut. Mit einem Ruck reisst sie sich los.

LILA Lech mich doch am Arsch!

Er stürzt sich erneut auf sie und bedrängt sie.

UNBEKANNTER Ich mag solche Schimpfworte, das erregt mich!

LILA Holen Sie sich gefälligst woanders einen runter! Und lassen Sie mich in Ruhe!

UNBEKANNTER Noch nicht. Erst will ich, dass du schreist.

LILA Sie tun mir weh.

UNBEKANNTER Oh, das tut mir aber leid!

LILA Sie haben so lange Fingernägel, Sie kratzen mich ja ganz blutig.

UNBEKANNTER Daran ist nur dein Fleisch schuld: es ist so weich.

LILA Um Gottes Willen!

Beim Wort "Gott" lässt er sie augenblicklich los.

UNBEKANNTER Entschuldigung, ich hab es nicht ernstgemeint, es war nur ein Scherz.

LILA Schöner Scherz. Sie haben mir fast den Arm gebrochen.

UNBEKANNTER Aber nein, das ist doch nur ein Kratzer … in Ordnung, ich werde meiner Maniküre sagen, sie soll mir die Krallen stutzen!

LILA Sie können Ihrer Maniküre von mir ausrichten, dass sie Sie zur Hölle schicken soll. *(Zu sich)* So ein Arschloch!

UNBEKANNTER Ich werd's ausrichten.

LILA Versuchen Sie nicht noch mal, mich anzurühren.

UNBEKANNTER Gut.

LILA Eigentlich sollte ich die Polizei rufen, sie haben mich ja regelrecht angegriffen!

UNBEKANNTER Nur ein bisschen, ein kleines bisschen.

LILA Wieso, Sie wären wohl noch weiter gegangen? Ihnen reichen wohl die Wunden noch nicht, die Sie auf meinem Arm zurückgelassen haben? Schauen Sie sich das mal an!

UNBEKANNTER Nehmen Sie es nicht so ernst. Das war nur ein Aufblitzen von Wahnsinn. Ich geb's ja zu, ich hätte mich beherrschen sollen, ich hätte nicht die Kontrolle verlieren dürfen, aber ein bisschen Schuld haben auch Sie …

LILA Ich?

UNBEKANNTER Ja, es ist Ihr Duft.

LILA Aber ich habe heute noch gar kein Parfüm aufgelegt.

UNBEKANNTER Es ist der Geruch ihres Körpers, verstehn Sie?

LILA Nein, das möchte ich lieber nicht verstehen.

UNBEKANNTER Sie riechen nach Fleisch … nach frishem Fleisch!

LILA Hören Sie, von jetzt an halten Sie Abstand. Bitte! Mindestens drei Schritte … *(zählt)* … verstanden?

UNBEKANNTER Intesi … versprochen!

LILA Also, wie Sie mich angeschaut haben! Sie hätten sich sehen sollen: erweiterte Pupillen und einen Blutstau hätten Sie, wie …
UNBEKANNTER Ein Tier?
LILA Genau. Woher …?
UNBEKANNTER … wisse ich das?
LILA Sie machen mir Angst.
UNBEKANNTER Na, endlich!
LILA Ach so! Das finden Sie wohl lustig?! Gut zu wissen. Man sollte sich davor hüten, jedem Dahergelaufenen über den Weg zu trauen.
UNBEKANNTER Hören Sie: es tut mir leid, wenn ich Sie erschreckt habe. Im Ernst!
LILA Und Sie glauben, dass Sie so billig davonkommen? Einfach mit 'ner Entschuldigung?
UNBEKANNTER Warum nicht? Im Grunde ist doch nichts passiert … nicht wirklich, meine ich.
LILA Und die Kratzer? Die hab ich wohl geträumt?
UNBEKANNTER Natürlich nicht.
LILA Sehen Sie? Es stimmt! Es ist wirklich etwas passiert, unbestreitbar …
UNBEKANNTER Eine Katze, die nicht im Arm gehalten werden wollte, mit ihren Krallen … das ist alles!
LILA Und diese Katze wären Sie?
UNBEKANNTER Warum nicht? Ich wäre gern eine Katze!
LILA Und ich soll wohl die Maus sein. Was?
UNBEKANNTER Nette Idee. Da bin ich gar nicht drauf gekommen. Ein Glück, dass Sie da sind!
LILA Sie werden noch im Gefängnis landen.
UNBEKANNTER Aber wo sind die Zeugen, die Beweise …
LILA Mein Wort gilt wohl nichts?
UNBEKANNTER Und das gynäkologische Gutachten? Die DNS Analyse?
LILA Ich muss mich wohl erst von Ihnen vergewaltigen lassen, um mein Recht zu bekommen?
UNBEKANNTER Dura lex sed lex!
LILA Sie kommen sich wohl sehr schlau vor? Sie wissen immer, wie man durchkommt. Sie kennen alle juristischen Tricks, um sich vor den Folgen zu drücken. Männer wie Sie müsste man schon als Kinder kastrieren! Oder ersäufen, vierteilen … Mistkerle!
UNBEKANNTER Jetzt übertreiben Sie aber! Da spricht das Ungeheuer aus Ihnen, wissen Sie das? Das in Ihnen nistet! Passen Sie bloss auf, dass Sie es nicht reizen! Denn wenn es erst mal ausbricht … dann gute Nacht!

LILA Das Ungeheuer, ich? Und Sie? Wer sind Sie überhaupt? Was haben Sie im Koffer? Nadeln, Ketten, Schlachterhaken … mein Gott, was rede ich da?

UNBEKANNTER Wieso interessiert Sie das? Weibliche Neugier?

LILA Haben Sie denn 'was zu verbergen?

UNBEKANNTER Und wenn ich Ihnen jetzt gestehen würde, dass da eine zerstückelte Frauenleiche drin ist? Was würden Sie dann machen? Um Hilfe rufen?

LILA Das möchte ich sehen!

UNBEKANNTER Wir sind hier völlig isoliert, noch dazu am Waldrand. Der Wind würde Ihre Stimme beiseite fegen wie … nichts … *(geht auf sie zu)*

LILA *(erschrocken)* Aber, Sie meinen das im Ernst!?

UNBEKANNTER Es ist doch völlig gleichgültig, ob ich die Wahrheit sage oder mir das ausdenke! Ausserdem, ist es nicht genau das, was du von mir wolltest?

LILA Ich?

UNBEKANNTER Ja Sie, genau Sie: mit Ihrer krankhaft provozierenden Art.

LILA Ich, krankhaft? Sie sind krankhaft!

UNBEKANNTER Hab ich Sie etwa gefragt, was Sie im Kühlschrank haben? Nein. Also ist mein Verhalten nicht krankhaft. Sie könnten neben dem Kalbsgulasch die Leiche eines Säuglings liegen haben, was weiss ich denn schon über Ihr Vorleben?

LILA Jetzt steigt der Druck an.

UNBEKANNTER Mir auch. Und zwar ziemlich heftig! Und daran sind nur Sie schuld und Ihre unterschwellige Boshaftigkeit. Ansteckend ist das, wissen Sie?

LILA Ich rede von der Kaffeemaschine. Da steigt der Druck, dio mio. In fünf Minuten kann ich Ihnen Ihren verdammten Kaffee machen. *(Drastisch)* Und basta! Dann gehen Sie wieder dahin, wo Sie hergekommen sind, verschwinden auf Nimmerwiedersehen. Haben wir uns verstanden?

UNBEKANNTER Wem sagen Sie das: ich kann es gar nicht abwarten, hier wegzukommen.

LILA Fünf Minuten, nur noch fünf Minuten.

UNBEKANNTER Eine Ewigkeit.

LILA Ach was, das ist doch gar nichts.

UNBEKANNTER Dreihundert Sekunden, wenn man es genau nimmt.

LILA Und das nennen Sie Ewigkeit?

UNBEKANNTER Die Wahrnehmung der Zeit ist etwas subjeltives. Manchmal scheint sie ganz schnell zu vergehen, manchmal überhaupt nicht. Jedenfalls vergeht sie nicht immer gleich schnell. Und vor allem nicht in der gleichen Richtung: mal geht sie vorwärts, mal rückwärts, es kommt ganz darauf an. Das nennt man die Richtung der Zeit. Sie folgt nämlich der Evolution des Universums, je nach dem, ob sie in die Zukunft oder in die Vergangenheit, projiziert ist. Die Theorie der Wiederkehr des Immergleichen, zum Beispiel … Nietzsche! Ein Wunder! Ein paar Umdrehungen weite, und schon ist der Übermensch da, ich meine natürlich den Mann mit Schwanz und Eiern … schwindelerregend!

LILA Wenn Sie glauben, dass Sie mich damit beeindrucken, dann müssen Sie miche für ganz schön blöd halten. Ich bin zwar ein einfaches Mädchen vom Land, gut, aber innerlich, tief in mir drin, da ist … ist …

UNBEKANNTER Ein Dämon?

LILA *(erschrickt)* Der Teufel!?

UNBEKANNTER Wenn Sie darauf bestehen …

LILA Nein, Sie bestehen mir ein bisschen zu sehr darauf? Sie haben gemerkt, dass ich Angst vor Ihnen habe und machen sich einen Spass drauss, mich zu schikanieren. Sie sind ein Sadist, ein Wahnsinniger, ein Ungeheuer!

UNBEKANNTER Vielleicht, weil ich lange Fingernägel habe?

LILA *(drohend)* Die hab ich auch! Ich kann mich ganz gut behaupten, da täuschen Sie sich mal nicht!

UNBEKANNTER Es wird ja behauptet, dass der Teufel ursprünglich eine Frau war und dass ihm die Eier erst später nachgewachsen sind, sozusagen als Schabernack der Natur. Dabei soll es sich um die sogenannte beschwanzte Frau handeln, oder, weniger ordinär, wie es unser Freund Freud ausgedrückt hat, um die phallische Frau. Als ob Sie, mit Verlaub! Eine Klitoris von der Grösse eines Penis hätten. Der Herr der Hölle und der Finsternis ist also nichts anderes als ein umgestülpter Schwanz. Die klassische Schlange, die sich in den Schwanz beisst … *(lacht)*

LILA L'astuto serpente … Die listige Schlange!

UNBEKANNTER Ja, Mozart *(singt die Arie der "Zauberflöte")* … Glauben Sie an den Teufel?

LILA Daran zu glauben wäre lächerlich, heutzutage.

UNBEKANNTER Aber nicht dran zu glauben kann gefährlich sein … sehr gefährlich.

LILA Ihrer Ansicht nach, gibt es ihn?

UNBEKANNTER Meiner Ansicht nach gibt es irgendwo so etwas. Ich kann Ihnen nicht sagen, wo, aber …

LILA Vielleicht im Zentrum der Erde … wie Ihr Metall … wie hiess das noch?

UNBEKANNTER Gallium. Aber Gallium ist kein Metall, sondern eine Legierung. Und das est ein ganz schöner Unterschied. Metall findet man nämlich in der Natur, Legierungen dagegen nicht: die muss man erst bilden, das heisst die Schöpfung ihrer selbst entziehen und sie dann neu erschaffen, wie der Teufel, wie die Hölle, die ja aus nichts als Elementen im Urzustand besteht, der Dschungel unseres Geistes, in dem unsere Phantasie manchmal ein bisschen wild herumspintisiert und dabei die menschlichen Grenzen überschreitet … uch langweile Sie?

LILA Dio mio!, Sie sprechen in Rätseln.

UNBEKANNTER Ja, ja, stimmt zuweilen wirkt das, was ich sage, ein wenig mysteriös, Signorina.

LILA Hört man denn, dass meine Muttersprache Italienisch ist? Mein Deutsch hinkt manchmal ein bisschen, ich weiss.

UNBEKANNTER Sie sprechen hervorragend Deutsch. Und Sie denken auch deutsch: genau wie Faust.

LILA Was meinen Sie damit?

UNBEKANNTER Damit meine ich, dass die Deutschen immer eine seltsame, etwas krankhafte Sympathie für das Böse gezeigt haben, über das ja vor der Gotik eigentlich nur gelacht wurde, geben wir es ruhig zu. Haben sie schon Vergil gelesen? In der Schule vielleicht …

LILA Vielleicht … aber ich glaube nicht …

UNBEKANNTER Also gut, jedenfalls sagt Vergil über die Hölle, wenn mich mein Gedächnis nicht täuscht, ungefähr: *Glücklich derjenige, der die Gesetze der Natur durchdringt, unnütze Vorurteile und Schrecken hinter sich lässt, den Styge, den Acheron, usw* … Aber ich langweile Sie!

LILA Ich kann jetzt sowieso nicht mehr schlagen. Und zu welchem Schluss kommt Ihr Vergil?

UNBEKANNTER *Die Türen und das Reich des Pluto, die Schicksalsschwelle und der fürchterliche Zerberus, das sind leere Worte, Kindermärchen, ein lästiges Traumgesicht.*

LILA Kindermärchen also. Ein lästiges Traumgesicht … es kommt mir so vor, als hätte ich Sie irgendwo schon einmal gesehen, als hätte ich Ihre Stimme schon mal gehört, als ob Ihr Gesicht und Ihre Worte etwas in mir zum Klingen bringen vielleicht ist es ja nur eine Ausgeburt meiner Ängste – also ob Sie die Inkarnation von irgendetwas sind, was mir wirklich zutiefst Angst macht.

UNBEKANNTER Was macht ihnen denn zutiefst Angst? Los, sprechen Sie es aus: ich platze vor Neugier!

LILA Der Tod vielleicht … nein, eigentlich mehr der Schmerz.

UNBEKANNTER Und die Sexualität, *jener heftig süsse Dominator der Tiegen meines Geistes, jenes furchtbare, doch s teure Geschenk des Himmels*, wie Leopardi es ausdrückt, sie macht Ihnen keine Angst?

LILA Ich finde, Sie gehen zu weit.

UNBEKANNTER Verzeihung, aber … Sie reagieren ziemlich gereizt! Das ist verdächtig, wissen Sie das?

LILA Panik, das ist nur die Panik.

UNBEKANNTER Unsinn, Sie brauchen keine Angst zu haben. Ich bin gar nicht so schlimm wie ich aussehe.

LILA Es ist beinahe so, alsob Sie die dunkelsten, mir selbst unbekannten Seiten jenes Unbewussten kennen würden, das mich immer wieder mit diesen Bildern vergewaltigt, die ich nicht sehen möchte ... ich kann es nicht besser erklären.

UNBEKANNTER Sie erklären das aber sehr gut. Wissen Sie: einem Kenner ...

LILA Ihre Physiognomie, jedenfalls, ist mir nicht neu; Ihre Stimme, die kommt mir vor, als ob es meine eigene wäre. *(zögert)* Seltsam ... *(schaut ihn an)* haben wir uns irgendwo schon einmal gesehen?

UNBEKANNTER Im Traum, vielleicht. Warum nicht? *(mit obszönem Beiklang)* Ich liebe es, in die Träume von Mädchen wie Sie einzudringen! Ein Genuss!

LILA Sie spielen mit dem Feuer.

UNBEKANNTER Sie auch.

LILA *(nach einer spannungsvollen Pause)* Dann sollten wir über solche Dinge eigentlich keine Witze machen.

UNBEKANNTER Da haben Sie recht. Träume, vor allem, wenn es sich um Alpträume bei Vollmond handelt, erforschen riskante Bereiche, off limits. Zutritt für Unbefugte verboten. Stimmt's? Privatgelände!

LILA *(lacht)* Achtung, bissiger Hund.

UNBEKANNTER Ein Hund mit drei Köpfen, richtig! Wie sind Sie jetzt darauf gekommen?

LILA *(harmlos)* Auf die drei Köpfe? *(Scherzhaft)* Wau, wau!

UNBEKANNTER *(im gleichen Ton)* Genau! Wau, wau!, macht Plutos Hund, der den Eingang zur Hölle bewacht. Wau, wau! Wau, wau!

LILA *(verschluckt sich)* Wau ... wa ...

Der Unbekannte beginnt, auf allen vieren herumzuspringen wie ein Hund.

UNBEKANNTER Wau, wau! Wau, wau! Wau, wau!

LILA *(erschrocken)* Genug ... genug jetzt! Hören Sie auf! Es ist genug! Basta!

UNBEKANNTER Das Gemeine an den Träumen ist immer, dass sie sich wie durch eine magische oder fast-nur-fast höllische Kraft konkretisieren.

LILA Lei è un sadico, ecco!

UNBEKANNTER Was haben Sie eigentlich gegen mich?

LILA Nichts … oder doch!, Sie sollen hier nicht den tollgewordenen Hund spielen. Nicht so echt, Sie sehen ja schon richtig aus wie ein wildegewordener Hund.

UNBEKANNTER Nein, nur ein schwarzes Pudelchen: das reicht, das ist mehr als genug.

LILA Ein Pudel!

UNBEKANNTER Na gut, ein kleines bisschen mephistophelisch.

LILA Ich bitte Sie, fangen Sie nicht wieder mit diesen *arkanischen* Andeutungen an … *(verwundert über sich selbst) Komisches* Wort … was ist denn das, *arkanisch?*

UNBEKANNTER Sie haben es doch gesagt!

LILA Ich habe es gesagt, ja, aber ich weiss überhaupt nicht, was es bedeutet.

UNBEKANNTER Nun sieh mal einer an! Wie kommt das bloss … ich habe aber Ihre Stimme gehört …

LILA Ich bin ein einfaches Mädchen, ich kenne solche Ausdrücke nicht … auf deutsch noch dazu … wo meine Muttersprache doch Italienisch ist … nein, nein, ich kann mit das nicht ausgedacht haben!

UNBEKANNTER Wer denn sonst? Der Teufel?

LILA Sie haben mir das ins Ohr gesetzt oder in den Mund gelegt.

UNBEKANNTER Wie soll ich das denn zuwege gebracht haben?

Sie will hinausgehen aber die Tür ist geschlossen.

LILA Weiss ich nicht. Sie sind ansteckend. Sie haben mich in diesen dialektischen Hinterhalt gelockt … sehen Sie, schon wieder ein Wort, das nicht von mir ist … und aus diesem Hinterhalt komme ich nicht mehr raus … Hilfe! Ich bin die Gefangene eines Ungeheuers.

UNBEKANNTER Innerlich oder äusserlich? Real oder imaginär? Konkret oder fantasmagorisch? Man muss es anfassen, um es zu glauben …

LILA Nein, rühren Sie mich nicht an!

UNBEKANNTER Sie haben wirklich den Teufel im Leib.

LILA Aber ich mach da nicht mit! Bei dem Spiel mach ich nicht mit, Sie Bastard!

UNBERKANNTER Sie werden schon mitmachen! Tun Sie doch nicht so spröde, Sie sind ja genau wie Margerita … *(er blickt sie an, als wolle er sie hypnotisieren, ihr Gesicht scheint von einem geheimnisvollen Licht erleuchtet)*

LILA Wer ist denn Margerita?

UNBEKANNTER Eine alte Bekannte von mir. Eine der zahllosen Freundinnen, die ich überall habe. Ein Seemann hat eine Braut in jedem

Hafen, das ist ja bekannt. Doch die arme Margerita ist leider von uns gegangen: für immer verloren, tot und begraben! Schade für sie ...
LILA *(erschrocken)* Woran ist sie denn gestorben?
UNBEKANNTER An einer schlimmen Krankheit: Liebe! ... Im Sinne von Beischlaf, das heisst, sie hat gerade gevögelt, gebumst, kopuliert (hat sich ficken lassen), kurzum, sie hat ihr Fleisch mit dem eines Ungeheuers vereinigt.
LILA Eines Ungeheuers?
UNBEKANNTER Ja! In Fleisch und Blut (vielleicht mehr Blut als Fleisch!) Ein alter Knacker, der sich als Jüngling verkleidet hatte, mit einem so grosse Schwanz *(zeigt die Grösse an)* und so einem kleinen Herzen ... *(zeigt, wie klein)* Verstehen Sie, was ich meine?
LILA Und sie hat dieses Arschloch geliebt?
UNBEKANNTER Entweder hasst man ein Ungeheuer oder man liebt es: einen Mittelweg gibt es nicht. Oder beides: aber total, bis zur Selbstaufgabe oder Verzweiflung, oder bis zur Erlösung des Ungeheuer – die ist aber immer ziemlich unwahrscheinlich. Denn wenn man erst einmal sehr tief gefallen ist, kommt man nur schwer wieder hoch.
LILA Sie sehen mich gerade so an, als ob Sie das Ungeheuer wären?
UNBEKANNTER Achten Sie einfach nicht drauf.
LILA Sie haben mich fast geblendet ... und ich soll nicht drauf achten?
UNBEKANNTER Das wae nur der Widerschein des Mondes, der immer mal wieder hinter den Nachtwolken auftaucht, die der Wing vor sich hertreibt.
LILA *(ironisch)* Wie poetisch Sie sind! Gleich kommt mir das Kotzen.
UNBEKANNTER Was sein muss, muss sein ... ausserdem, meine Liebe, heutzutage geht alles so drunter und drüber, als ob gar nicht mehr existierte, und doch ... Sie verstehen mich? *(zweideutig)*
LILA Oh nein!
UNBEKANNTER Oh doch! Deswegen brauchen wir nämlich die Poesie! Nur sie ist noch in der Lage, das Wesentliche in all seinen Nuancen festzuhalten, und die Dinge zu sublimieren. Damit das Chaos, in dem wir alle stecken, nicht zur Dreigroschenorgie abwirtschaftet, bei der die Erregung gerade dreimal für einen müden Orgasmus reicht, so kümmerlich wie der Nieser eines kleinen Jungen beim Popeln.
LILA Si vergogni! Sie sollten sich schämen!
UNBEKANNTER Zum Glück gibt es die Poesie. Damit ist das gute Gewissen gerettet, das Gehör in Ordnung, und die Zunge schlägt nicht dauernd an den schmerzenden Zahn. Mit einer gigantischen verbalen Onanie löst sich das alles in eitles Wohlgefallen auf. Zufrieden?
LILA Das kann Ihnen doch egal sein: mit Ihnen spreche ich überhaupt nicht mehr. Sie sind mir zu ordinär ...

UNBEKANNTER Sie brauchen nichts zu befürchten: gleich wird es Tag. Und alles hat ein Ende.

LILA Wirklich?

UNBEKANNTER Ja, ja, Sie werden sehen: die bösen Träume lösen sich in Nichts auf.

LILA Und Sie machen sich wieder auf die Reise? Da werde ich aber aufatmen.

UNBEKANNTER Für Sie bin ich wohl ein richtiger Alptraum, danke, keine Ursach. Jedenfall: wenn die Sonne aufgeht, (wenn sie aufgeht) werde ich mich verdünnisieren. Ich verspreche es Ihnen. Und was ich verspreche, halte ich.

LILA Wenn sie aufgeht?

UNBEKANNTER Das ist nur eine Hypothese.

LILA In dem Sinne, dass sie vielleicht nicht aufgehen könnte?

UNBEKANNTER Unsinn, halten Sie mich für einen Idioten? Glauben Sie, ich weiss nicht, dass die Sonne früher oder später unbedingt aufgehen muss, so wie sie es seit hunderten von Millionen Jahren tut?

LILA Was wollen Sie also damit sagen?

UNBEKANNTER Dass einer von uns beiden das Aufgehen der Sonne nicht mehr erleben könnte. Der Gedanke ist Ihnen wohl noch gar nicht gekommen?

LILA Aber wenn es doch nur noch wenige Minuten sind … *(ihr kommt ein entsetzlicher Zweifel)* Oder Sie vielleicht in Mörder?

UNBEKANNTER Meine Liebe!, der schlimmste Mörder, unser schlimmster Feind, ist das Schicksal. Alles wird vom Schicksal bestimmt. Ich hab damit gar nichts zu tun. Ich gehorche lediglich. Gehorche und kämpfe. Manches verstehe ich nicht ganz, aber ich passe mich an. Kurzum: wenn ich sterben muss, dann muss ich eben sterben. Und das gleiche gilt für Sie.

LILA Für mich?

UNBEKANNTER Natürlich: wenn zum Beispiel das Schicksal entschieden hat, dass Sie in zehn Sekunden sterben werden, nehmen wir mal an, an einem Herzschlag, was können Sie schon dagegen tun? Rebellieren? Kämpfen? Versuchen Sie's doch mal! Los, zeigen Sie's mir … winden Sie sich, wackeln Sie mit dem Hintern, gehen Sie aus sich raus: dreschen Sie los, verhauen Sie mich, los, hierher, ich bin das Schicksal, kratzen Sie mich, versuchen Sie, mir zu widerstehen! Sehen Sie, es geht nicht?

LILA Ich soll sterben? In zehn Sekunden?

UNBEKANNTER … zehn, neun, (da können Sie mal sehen, wie in gewissen Momenten die Zeit davonfliegt!) … sechs, fünf … (was ist schon eine Sekunde? Scheinbar gar nichts, und doch kommen jede Sekunde

Millionen, Milliarden von Mikroorganismen zur Welt und sterben wieder!)
… drei, zwei, eins, null! Sind Sie in Ordnung?
LILA Ich glaube, ja … Ich hoffe!
UNBEKANNTER Dann hat das Schicksal noch nicht über Ihr Los
entschieden. Im übrigen man auch das Gegenteil nicht herbeizwingen. Weil
nämlich die Parzen, die in der Unterwelt am Leben der Menschen spinnen,
einfach ihre Productionszeit einhalten müssen: es sind nur drei für das
gesamte Menschengeschlecht! Das verstehen Sie sicher!
LILA Ich würde Ihnen gern eine in Ihre widerliche Fresse schlagen.
UNBEKANNTER Nur zu, machen Sie sich über mich lustig. Oder
hätten Sie es lieber, wenn ich verschwinde, so wie der Traum beim
Erwachen: einmal die Augen gerieben, eine Tasse Kaffee … ach ja, … wa
macht eigentlich der Kaffee?
LILA Kommt sofort. Wenn Sie endlich aufhören zu quatschen?
UNBEKANNTER Ich bis eben, zu Ihrem Unglück, kein Traum.
Vielleicht ein Märchenwesen, aber aud Fleisch und Blut, kein Traum …
LILA Mein Gott, ich ertrage Sie nicht mehr!
UNBEKANNTER *(nachgiebig)* Ich bitte Sie, sprechen Sie seinen Namen
nicht so leichtfertig aus. Ein bisschen mehr Respekt, wenn ich bitten darf!
Wenn schon nicht für Ihn, dann wenigstens für mich!
LILA *(wie besessen)* Manchmal glaube ich, in dem, was Sie sagen, einen
Schimmer von Wahrheit zu erkennen, doch dann entgleitet mir wieder alles,
ich verliere mich und weiss nicht, was icht tun soll, um mich wieder zu
fangen …
UNBEKANNTER Das sollten Sie aber wissen. Denken Sie mal darüber
nach …
LILA Ich weiss nicht. Es kommt darauf an, worüber!
UNBEKANNTER Über das, was sich da in Ihrem Hirn so bewegt: und
was gelegentlich aus den Abgründen Ihres Unbewussten hochkommt wie
eine unterirdische Welle, die an der Küste Ihres Ichs zerschellt und dabei
Tropfen heissen Lavas in die Gegend spritzt.
LILA Dabei ist Ihre Psy … Psyche (schon wieder so ein Wort, das ich far
nicht kenne) ist viel kaputter als meine!
UNBEKANNTER Total kaputt, ich geb's zu. Wenn Sie versuchen
würde, die Knoten meiner verknäulten Seele zu lösen, würden Sie sich
hoffnungslos verstricken und mit in die Tiefe gezogen werden, in genau
jenen gigantischen Wirbel, in dem Sie gerade eben im Traum … diese
Bestie gesehen haben!
LILA Diese verfluchte Bestie' Sie verdammter Kerl!
UNBEKANNTER Glauben Sie mir, ein bisschen Selbstkontrolle täte
Ihnen ganz gut – hoffentlich befolgen Sie diesen Rat. Man sollte das eigene
Ich unter Verschluss halten wie in einem Kloster.

LILA Oder wie den Inhalt Ihres Koffers. Es würde mich wirklich interessieren ...

UNBEKANNTER Nein, machen Sie den nicht auf, machen Sie den nie auf: sie sollten diesen Koffer betrachten wie Ihre Seele: was da drin ist, könnte Sie bei Tageslicht vernichten.

LILA Davvero?

UNBEKANNTER Sie ahnen ja nicht, wieviele unangenehme Überraschungen da zum Vorschein kämen ...

LILA Aus dem Koffer? Eine Metallegierung, haben Sie gesagt, hergestellt in einem von diesen blöden Militärlabors, wo sich Leute ungeheuerliche, unvorstellbare Sachen ausdenken ...

UNBEKANNTER Schon gut, schon gut ...

LILA Oder ist da noch was anderes?

UNBEKANNTER Ihr Kopf scheint eine regelrechte Fabrik für Explosivstoffe zu sein. Da reicht ein Funke, um eine Kettenreaktion mit katastrophalen Auswirkungen auszulösen. Eine richtige Pandorabüchse, glauben Sie mir.

LILA Sie wollen mich wohl schon wieder in Angst und Schrecken versetzen.

UNBEKANNTER Ich kann Sie nur inständig bitten, sich nicht in Angst und Schrecken versetzen zu lassen. Es lohnt sich nicht. Wir sitzen auf der Atombombe? Na und? Solange sie nicht explodiert, können wir es ruhig miteinander treiben, wenn wir Lust dazu haben. Das Ungehuer in uns? Es reicht, dass es sich in einer Ecke zusammenkauert und uns mit seinem Gejaule nicht auf den Wecker geht. Was ist überhaupt, letztes Endes, die Existenz? Doch nur ein Splitter, der, losgelöst, für den Bruchteil eines Augenblicks in der Nacht der Zeiten umherirrt. Wozu sich das Leben ruinieren, es ist ohnehin kurz genug. Denken Sie einfach nicht mehr dran.

LILA Woran soll ich nicht mehr denken?

UNBEKANNTER Wie, woran? An das Ungeheuer natürlich!

LILA Mal brüllt es, mal heult es wie eine ausgehungerte Hyäne, manchmal fletscht es die Zähne, als ob es jeden Augenblick losschlagen wolle: bisschen schwierig, nicht daran zu denken!

UNBEKANNTER Stellen Sie sich vor, Ihr Geist sei wie mein Koffer, ja? Das heisst leer, solange wir nicht – ich in meinen Koffer und sie in Ihr Hirn – etwas hineintun. Können Sie mir folgen?

LILA Vielleicht ... vielleicht bin ich dem ganzen nicht gewachsen ... ich bin nur ein böses, ein ungezogenes Kind ... weiter nichts ... was verlange Sie von mir? Wie können Sie annehmen, dass ich da mitkomme, mit einem ... mit einem ...

UNBEKANNTER Mit einem Teufel?

LILA Ja, ja, Verzeihung.

UNBEKANNTER Nicht nötig. Jeder sieht die Dinge auf seine Weise. Und wenn Sie mich unbedingt für den Teufel halten wollen, na gut, dann tu ich Ihnen eben den Gefallen. Zufrieden?

LILA Ich wünschte, ich hätte Sie nie kennengelernt, ich wünschte, Sie hätten sich weit weg von hier verirrt, Sie hätten das Licht nicht gesehen und deshalb auch nicht gewusst, dass ich gerade am Aufmachen war, ich wünschte, die Jäger kämen zum Frühstück …

UNBEKANNTER Sie vergessen eins in Ihre blöden Litanei. *(Imitiert ihre Stimme)* Ich wünschte, dass es das Ungeheuer nicht gäbe oder dass es wenigstens nicht solche Untaten begangen hätte. Richtig?

LILA Sie wollen wohl, dass ich vor Angst sterbe?

UNBEKANNTER Ach, Sie haben Angst?

LILA Und ob! Angst vor mir selbst. Davor, was ich getan habe oder was ich tun könnte oder was ich tun werde, ich weiss, dass ich es am Ende tun werde. Deshalb tobt diese Angst in mir und will heraus, wie der Schaum aus einer Bierflasche, die geschüttelt worden ist und alles drumherum nasspritzt!

UNBEKANNTER Das sind Symptome des Übels, das Sie in sich ausbrüten. An der Wurzel sitzt das Ungeheuer. Statt zu wissen, sollten Sie lieber intuitiv reagieren, denn das volle, das vollständige Bewusstsein von sich selbst kann einen auch – fst unvermeidlich ist das – in abgrunditiefe Verzweiflung stürzen. Es ist sicher nicht einfach, unbewusst zu handeln, intuitiv zu sein, aber immer noch möglich. Verstehen, ohne wirklich zu verstehen … um, aufgepasst!, das Tier, das wir selbst sind, zu zerstören, ohne gleichzeitig um nichts und wieder nichts unsere Seele in Stücke zu hauen. Sie werden mich fragen: wie? Gut, dafür bin ich ja da. Lassen Sie mich einen Augenblick nachdenken, dann werden Sie sehen!

LILA *(nach einer kurzen Pause)* Sie stellen sich gerade eine nackte Frau, vor? Nicht? Das bin ich! Ich liebkose mich, obwohl ich es gar nicht will, so ein Schweinkram! Was tue ich da in Ihrer Phantasie?

UNBEKANNTER Jeder konzentriert sich auf seine Weise. Der eine raucht eine Zigarette, der andere … also, mischen Sie sich nicht in meine erotischen Phantasien ein. Ich werde wohl dei Freiheit haben …

LILA Aber wie ist es nur möglich, dass ich in Sie hineinblicken kann! Oder in mich?

UNBEKANNTER Ruhe!

LILA Mein Gott! Sie denken in mir! Sie denken für mich in mir!

UNBEKANNTER Ruuuhee!

Er ist um Konzentration bemüht. Doch hat dieser Versuch eine ganze Reihe von seltsamen Nebeneffekten der paranormalen Art, z.B. Geräusche, ein merkwürdiges Leuchten, Bolder, die blitzschnell auf den Wänden eerscheinen, Schatten, schliesslich die

UNBEKANNTER Haben Sie das gesehen? Gehört? Wahrgenommen? Hat es Ihnen gefallen?

LILA Und ich soll … diese Abscheulichkeiten … in … mir?

UNBEKANNTER Es ist noch viel schlimmer: ich habe nur ganz en passant ein paar verstreute Brocken zusammengetragen. Sagen wir: das Beste aus Ihrer Produktion. Goethe hätte tausend Seiten dafür gebraucht (so lange wie für seinen Homunculus!), ich dagegen interessiere mich mehr für das Ausgefallene: nur wenige Worte, ich lasse die Fakten sprechen. Denn man hat ja schon manchmal Lust zu lesen, aber es muss doch in Rahmen bleiben, nicht wahr …

LILA Hilflos fühle ich mich mir selbst ausgeliefert …

UNBEKANNTER Und deshalb weinen Sie? Übertreiben Sie nicht ein bisschen? Es stimmt zwar, dass schlimmste Übel von uns selbst ausgeht, aber es gibt für alles ein Mittel, glauben Sie nicht?

LILA Nein, das glaube ich nicht.

UNBEKANNTER Sie brauchen nicht zu verzweifeln. Im Grunde ist Ihr Inneres auch nicht finsterer oder barbarischer als das von Ihresgleichen. Wenn man ein bisschen gräbt, stösst man bei jedem Menschen irgendwann auf die Steinzeit, sieh mal einer an! Ich frage mich, wieso? Habt Ihr nicht Riesenfortschritte gemacht in … wieviele Jahre sind es eigentlich?, also, ich kann sie jetzt nicht zählen, in vielleicht dreitausend Jahren Geschichte? Und trotzdem seid ihr so primitiv geblieben wie Höhlenmenschen.

LILA Ich nicht! Ich nicht, jedenfalls ist mir bis heute nicht der Gedanke gekommen, das ich so sein soll wie Sie es beschreiben.

UNBEKANNTER Wäre es vielleicht besser gewesen, wenn Sie weiter ohne dieses Bewusstsein geblieben wären, so wie die "drei Äffchen" aus dem Märchen? Wenn das Ich nicht hört, was das Es sagt, und das Es nicht sieht, was das Gewissen tut, und das Gewissen zu dem schweigt, was die beiden anderen tun, dann geht es uns besser als im Paradies, das können Sie mir glauben.

LILA Ich habe furchtbare Angst. Hören Sie auf!

UNBEKANNTER Aber es sind Ihre angeborenen Ängste, die solche Gedanken hervorbringen – und die wiederum konkretisieren sich in Bildern, werden zu Fleisch und bahnen dann der Fleischeslust den Weg (ob wir wollen oder nicht, wir landen immer wieder beim Fleisch, das zwar schwach sein mag, aber so gut!), jetzt habe ich den Faden verloren, was wollte ich sagen …?

LILA Meine angeborenen Ängste …

UNBEKANNTER Ach ja, richtig. Im Laufe der Nacht sind diese Ängste zu Ungeheuern geworden, die sich wie riesige Schatten auf die Wände Ihres Ichs projiziert haben. So wie eine Ameise, die durch die Linse eines Projektors läuft: auf der Leinwand erscheint dann ein prähistorisches Ungeheuer, eine infernalische Kreatur, und in Ihrer Einfalt werden Sie denken, dem Teufel persönlich begegnet zu sein! Doch in Wirklichkeit, na? Was war es?

LILA Nichts.

UNBEKANNTER Genau: nichts! Das gleiche gilt für die Alpträuyme, die im Schlaff fst unerträglich wirken und die man beim Aufwachen am liebsten aus dem Hirn auslöschen möchte. Aber was sind sie denn in Wirklichkeit, doch nur ein winziger Bruchteil unseres nächtlichen Nirwana. Und für die paar Zehntelsekunden, in denen unser Hirn eine seltsame Wendung nimmt, sollen wir uns das Leben zur Hölle machen, nein, da werden die Flügel eingezogen, und der Asphalt brennt schon, noch bevor wir auf's Gaspedale gedrückt haben.

LILA Ich weiss es nicht … ich weiss nicht, was ich machen soll!

UNBEKANNTER Ich hab es doch gerade gesagt: nichts. Lassen Sie die flüchtigen Schatten ruhen, das sind Luftgespinste des Unendlichen, abstrakte Bilder am bleiernen Himmel der Seele, die dich manchmal schon in der Wiege ersticken wollen (ja, ja, ich bin auch mal ein Kind gewesen. Und ich kann mich genau an die Todesangst jener Zeiten erinnern, als ich mich noch im vorbewussten, im "tierischen" Stadium befand, als das Gewissen als solches noch nicht angeknipst und die Seele noch ein leerer Behälter war); und andere Bilder wiederum können dich in himmlische Sphären versetzen, in den geistigen Rausch eines inner Sublimationsprozesses. Mit unseren Visionen ist es ein wenig wie mit dem Wein, der mit den Jahren reifer wird, der sich vom Most in Nektar verwandelt, der göttlich ist und dämonisch zugleich, weil es Gott nicht ohne seinen Gegenspieler, den Dämon geben kann. Und umgekehrt.

LILA Wenn er nur nicht zu Essig wird, dieser Wein.

UNBEKANNTER Das liegt nur an uns, das ist doch der Punkt.

LILA Jetzt erklären Sie mir mal, wie Sie es anstellen, in meine Hirnwindungen zu gelangen.

UNBEKANNTER Oh, nein, das ist nicht so, wofür halten Sie mich? Erstens kann ich das gar nicht. Und zweitens, warum sollte ich das tun?

LILA *(aggressiv)* Also, dann verstehe ich nicht, was hier los ist.

UNBEKANNTER Sie denken nur das weiter, was ich sage. Sie stellen sich das im gleichen Moment vor, in dem ich es ausspreche und glauben deshalb, dass ich Ihnen die Ideen absauge, wie ein Vampir oder ein Blutegel *(versucht, sie auf den Hals zu küssen),* und dann gibt es einen Knutschfleck …

LILA *(entwindet sich ihm)* Und wie erklären Sie sich das?

UNBEKANNTER Ich erkläre mir gar nichts: ich sage doch nur ganz triviale, banale, selbstverständliche Dinge. Sie denken nur, dass Sie das denken, was ich denke und dass ich das denke, was Sie denken. Aber nur, weil ich ziemlich allgemeingültige Gedanken ausspreche. UNIVERSELL nennt man so was! Das heisst, gültig für die gesamte Menschheit.

LILA Sie haben es gut.

UNBEKANNTER Sie können ganz beruhigt sein. Ich bin bei weitem nicht so dialibosch wie ich aussehe.

LILA Kann sein … Sie hinken aber!

UNBEKANNTER Ich? Wirklich? Das habe ich noch gar nicht gemerkt. Ich werde mir mal die Hufe kontrollieren lassen,

LILA Ausserdem ist Ihr linker Fuss grösser als der rechte: Ihnen platzt ja der Schuh.

UNBEKANNTER Das ist der Fuss, mit dem ich immer auf's Gaspedal trete: vielleicht bin ich in letzter Zeit ein bisschen zuviel Auto gefahren … *(zieht sich den Schuh aus, ein monströser Fuss kommt zum Vorschein)*

LILA Wo andere einen Fuss haben, Sie einen Ziegenhuf!

UNBEKANNTER Na und? *(Zieht sich rasch den Schuh wieder an)* Sie sind ganz schön rassistisch. Sie haben wohl was gegen Leute, die ein bisschen anders sind? Gucken Sie doch mal in den Spiegel: Sie haben auch ein hässliches Muttermal auf dem Hals. Der guten Manieren wegen habe ich bischer so getan, als ob ich es nicht sehe. Machen wir doch folgendes: wenn Sie bein Dermatologen Ihr Muttermal untersuchen lassen, gehe ich zum Schuhmacher!

LILA Machen Sie sich nur lustig über mich: ich habe mich wahrscheinlich geirrt.

UNBEKANNTER Ja, es ist ja auch noch ziemlich dunkel … Und die Phantasie hat Ihnen einen Schabernack gespielt. Sie sehen aber auch überall Ungeheuer, das scheint eine fixe Idee von Ihnen zu sein! Dabei habe ich mich doch bis jetzt ziemlich wie ein Kavalier benommen (abgesehen von den Kratzern auf dem Arm, das war ein kleiner Rückfall ins Animalische, wie er mich von Zerit zu Zeit befällt), obwohl ich die Situation hier durchaus dazu ausnutzen könnte, um meine niederen Gelüste zu befriegen. Wenn mir welche kommen, heisst das, aber es ist nicht gesagt, dass mir keine kommen. Ich glaube aber, dass ich sie eigentlich ganz gut unter Kontrolle habe. Oder etwa nicht?

LILA *(geht nervös zum Fenster)* Wo nur die Sonne bleibt! Diese Nacht ist so kalt und dauert eine Ewigkeit!

Hinter ihrem Rücken und von ihr unbemerkt, schüttet der Unbekannte schnell zwei Flaschen Grappa in sich hinein und stopft sich den Mund mit allem möglichen Essbaren

UNBEKANNTER Wenn Sie erlauben: Ewigkeit ist eine abstrakte Grösse, wieder mal so ein zweideutiges Produkt des menschlichen Gesistes, der in seiner Begrenztheit und Zufälligkeit ad hoc hypothetisch eine nichtexistente Unendlichkeit annimmt. Als ob die Unendlichkeit eine einfache Abfolge von geometrischen (oder mathematischen) Punkten sei, ein Goldesel, der unaufhörlich Geld kackt! So ist es aber nicht! Es ist ein grosser Fehler, die Ewigkeit nur quantitativ und nicht qualitativ zu bewerten. Ewig ist der Augenblick, nicht alle Augenblicke zusammengenommen. Die Unendlichkeit zu erreichen bedeutet, zum Augenblick, zum Moment, wie Faust, zu sagen: "Oh Augenblick, verweile!" und nicht stattdessen: "Oh Langeweile, vergeh so schnell due kannst!". Nehmen Sie mich, zum Beispiel, auch ich bin hier vorbeigekommen und, von einer unwiderstehlichen Kraft angezogen – der Lust auf einen Kaffee – habe ich angehalten. Und jetzt warte ich schon eine Ewigkeit darauf!

LILA Wo kommen Sie eigentlich her?

UNBEKANNTER Wollen Sie das wirklich wissen? *(anzüglich)* Ich komme von einem Ort, den Sie nicht kennen … und ich bin ganz sicher, dass Sie ihn auch nicht kennenlernen wollen. Also … hören Sie auf. Das ist besser. Besser für Sie!

LILA Auf der anderen Seite der Grenze?

UNBEKANNTER Viel weiter.

LILA Ziemlich geheimnisvoll!

UNBEKANNTER Was ist das Leben schon ohne Geheimnis?

LILA Gar nichts. Da heben Sie recht.

UNBEKANNTER Genau wie ein Essen ohne Salz … Jetzt muss ich aber pinkeln … Verzeihung! Wo ist das Klo?

LILA Ganz nach hinten durch und dann links … Warten Sie, es ist abgeschlossen. Ich muss Ihnen den Schlüssel geben … verdammt … *(wühlt in einer Schublade herum)* wo hab ich ihn nur hingetan?

UNBEKANNTER Beeilen Sie sich, ich bin ein bisschen schwach auf der Blasé.

LILA Ich kann ihn nicht finden … *(sucht)* wir schliessen die Toilette immer ab, damit sich nicht irgendwelche Fixer dort ihren Schuss setzen … die Drogen sind leider inzwischen auch bis hierher vorgedrungen … arme Kerle sind das!

UNBEKANNTER Also, mir sind sie scheissegal!

LILA Ich hab ihn gefunden …

UNBEKANNTER *(reisst ihr den Schlüssel aus der Hand)* Geben Sie schon her … *(geht in die falsche Richtung)*

LILA Links, habe ich gesagt, sinistra! Sind Sie taub?

UNBEKANNTER *(rüttelt nervös an der Türklinke)* Verdammt nochmal, jetzt bin ich in der Küche gelandet … ich gehe immer nach dem Geruch, wissen Sie? In dieser Wirtschaft stinkt es aus der Küche mehr als aus dem Klo.

LILA *(alleingeblieben)* Allein mit diesem Wahnsinnigen! Was der alles redet … brr, ich habe eine richtige Gänsehaut! *(blickt forschend durch das Fenster)* Und ausgerechnet heute kommt keiner, noch nicht einmal der mit dem Kaffee "wie immer" (mit einem Schuss Cognac, ber … pssst!, das darf man am frühen Morgen nicht so laut sagen). Sonst klopft der um die Zeit immer ans Fenster und lässt sich das Tablett nach draussen reichen, damit er sich nicht die Jacke ausziehen und den Hund anbinden muss (hier lasse ich diese sabbernden Köter nämlich nicht rein) das Ungeheuer … das fehlte uns gerade noch, das Ungeheuer! Dabei gehen die Geschäfte auch so schon schlecht genug.

Die Tür der Toilette wird aufgerissen. Lila bemerkt das nicht und schaut weiter aus dem Fenster. Sie wartet, dass jemand kommt. Der Unbekannter versucht zu urinieren. Das Geräusch des Pinkelns wird immer lauter, "diabolischer!, am Ende klingt es wie ein Wasserfall. Die Wasserspülung erzeugt einen graunhaften Lärm. Lila ärgert sich über diesen Krach.

LILA Der bleibt aber lange da drin … vielleicht ist ihm schlecht?

UNBEKANNTER Ist es schon Tag?

LILA Noch nicht … *(zu sich)* seltsam … *(zu ihm)* ist etwas?

UNBEKANNTER Mir geht's ausgezeichnet, Sie brauchen sich keine Sorgen zu machen. Ich hab nur so viele Knöpfe zuzumachen … mein Anzug ist ein bisschen altmodisch … eine Art Rüstung, manch einem kommt et wie eine Kostümierung vor, aber mir gefällt. Ausserdem ist er bequem … nur nicht, wenn man den Pillermann rausholen will! Aber Sie haben solche Probleme ja nicht … rein jetzt, du Bestie!

LILA Mit wem streiten Sie denn?

UNBEKANNTER Mit einem Freund.

Aus der Kloschüssel steigt ein seltsamer roter Dampf, der allmählich die ganze Toilette einnebelt. Das Ganze ist von seltsamen Geräuschen begleitet: Gewimmer, Geheul, Geschrei, dazu eine "höllische" Beleuchtung. Plötzlich dreht der Unbekannter sich um und zeigt seine wahrhafte Teufelsgestalt: er hat einen Eselskopf mit bluttriefenden Hörnern.

UNBEKANNTER Ich bin die dunkle Seite des Lichts, ich hebe den Blick auf zu Gott und scheue mich nicht, ihm die nackte Wahrheit zu sagen. Dem Gott, der der Menschheit sieben Plagen auferlegte, dem Gott, der Abraham das unmenschliche Opfer seines erstgeborenen Sohnes abverlangte, dem Gott, der seine eigene Kreatur, Fleisch seines Geistes, zum Tod am Kreuze zwang und der, um der Sucht nach Ewigkeit Einhalt zu gebieten, dem Menschen nur eine einzige Erbschaft hinterliess: den Tod, im Tausch mit einem Leben im Jenseits das es nicht gibt, denn nicht einmal das Diesseits existiert, und ihr haltet ihn immer noch für den Ewigen Vater? Nun gut, denn jener Gott bin ich, Baphomet, und es gibt keinen anderen Gott neben mir! Es ist die reine Verarschung, den Menschen glauben zu machen, es gäbe ein Wesen jenseits von Gut und Böse, die endgültige Wahl zu haben, als liege die Entscheidung bei ihm.
Oh, Mensch, was bist du für ein armer Tor, einen enzigen Biss nur hat die Schlange dir zugestanden: als du dich auf dieses gefährliche Spiel eingelassen hast mit demselben Schöpfer, der dich gerade so wie ein Spielzeug in den Garten der Welt gesetzt hat, um ab und zu eine Kegelpartie zu machen, unnütz hast du das Leben dir schwer gemacht.
Ich, ich, ich, ich allein bin dein Gott!
Und es gibt keinen anderen Gott neben mir!

(Mit einem Lächeln) Gezeichnet: Baphomet!

Wie ein Echo hört man das Geheul der Wölfe, unter denen man deutlich eine Stimme heraushört.

DIE KLAGE DES EINSAMEN WOLFES

Der Mensch ist des Menschen Wolf,
kein anderes Tier ist schlimmer als er.
Von Abfall muss ich mich nähren,
während er auf alles schiesst, was fliegen kann.

Nach seinem Bilde hat ihn Gott erschaffen,
doch später erst das wahre Wesen
seiner Seele enthüllt: er hat sich in den Teufel
verwandelt, von dem er glaubte, er sei anders als er selbst.

Doch welche Ungeheuer sind im Dunkel verborgen,
die nicht Produkte seiner Phantasie sind?
Die Schatten auf den Mauern sind der pure Wahnsinn,

die die Wirklichkeit in Wahn verwandelt.

Nimm dich in acht, LILA,
vor dem schrecklichen Ungeheuer,
das in dir versteckt ist,
mit allen Kräften musst du es bekämpfen,
wenn du nicht besessen werden willst.

LILA *(der das Wolfsgeheul auf die Nerven geht)* Verdammte Köter! Die haben mir gerade noch gefehlt, wo ich sowieso schon vor Angst fast vergehe! Wenn es draussen friert, nähern sie sich den bewohnten Gebieten und suchen zwischen den Abfällen nach Fressbarem. Das sind keine Wölfe mehr, Schakale sind das geworden, widerliche Geschöpfe, entartet, Zombies, schlüpfriger und unberechenbarer als Schlangen! Und je mehr Hunger sie haben, desto frecher werden sie, richtig unverschämt, sie fordern sogar die Jäger heraus und versuchen, in die Häuser einzudringen … manchmal nehmen sie sogar Menschengestalt an, uns zwar so, dass man sie in der Dunkelheit kaum erkennen kann, mit ihren langen Zähnen und haarigen Ohren … dem da traue ich auch nicht über den Weg. Was der redet! Und was der für ein finsteres Gesicht hat! Und wen er ein Wolf ist, ich meine, das Ungeheuer? Wer weiss, was der wirklich im Koffer hat … *(zieht den Koffer ins Licht)* Meine Güte, der wiegt bestimmt einen Zentner! Aber nicht doch, Lila, hör auf mit deinen Phantastereien, was du für hässlicht Gedanken hast! Was soll schon drin sein … ein Gelehrter wird er sein, und das sind seine Bücher … gut, aber warum lässt er sie dann nicht im Auto? Und die Geschichte mit diesem Gallier oder wie das heisst, Gallium! Das glaub ich sowieso nicht! Ich bin doch nicht blöd! *(plötzlich kommt ihr ein Zweifel)* Und wenn er doch das Ungeheuer ist, und da ist wirklich eine Leiche drin, die zerstückelte Leiche seines letzten Opfers? Nein, das kann nicht sein … dann müsster er voller Blut sein …? Santo Dio! Ich muss das unbedingt wissen. Weil, wenn er ein Ungeheuer, ein richtiges Ungeheuer wäre, cine Art Wolf, dann könnte ich sein nächstes Opfer sein. Wer weiss, was dem in den Sinn kommt … ausserdem, was ist schon dabei, wenn ich mal einen Blick hineinwerfe, nur um mich zu vergewissern, mit wem ich es zu tun habe … aber du musst schnell machen, Lila, schnell … bevor er zurückkommt …

Hinter ihr kommt der Unbekannter heraus, wieder normal. Er schaut stumm und ohne sich bemerkbar zu machen, mit zufriedenem Grinsen der Szene zu, fast, als ob es ihm recht wäre, dass Lila in seinen Sachen herumwühlt. LILA lässt die beiden Schlösser aufschnappen und murmelt:

LILA Strano, der ist offen …

Dann macht sie ganz langsam den Koffer auf, als befürchte sie, dass irgendetwas Schreckliches herausspringen könnte. Ganz langsam hebt sie den Deckel hoch. Ihr Gesicht wird von einem seltsamen blutroten Licht aus dem Koffer beleuchtet, aus dem sich auch stinkende, farbige Dämpfe erheben. Lila verharrt einen Augenblick und betrachtet entsetzt den Inhalt des Koffers. Mit einem Schlag und einem Schrei klappt sie ihn wieder zu.

LILA Neeeiiin!
UNBEKANNTER Na?! Hat Ihnen das Spektakel gefallen, mein Fräulein? Was hattest du denn gehofft, darin zu finden? Blumen vielleicht?
LILA Sein Blick …! Wieso hab ich das nicht gleich begriffen, wer sich hinter solch schmutzigen Reden verbirgt … das Ungeheuer, der Wahnsinnige! La Bestia!
UNBEKANNTER Sprechen Sie es ruhig aus: der Phychopath! Ich bin nicht so schnell beleidigt.
LILA Rühren Sie mich nicht an, kommen Sie nicht näher! Hilfe!
UNBEKANNTER Deine Schuld. Du hast es selbst gewollt. Musstest du unbedingt deine Nase in meinen Koffer stecken? Jetzt ist es, als hättest du da, wo dein Gewissen noch wie ein Verschluss funktionierte, den Deckel heruntergenommen: pumm, und der Sekt, der Nektar der Götter und der Dämonen ist rausgeschäumt, weil du ihn eigenhändig geschüttelt hast. Dabei hast du dir die Händchen schmutzig gemacht, wie mit dem Samen des Ungeheuers. Und jetzt kannst du es geniessen.
LILA Widerlich!
UNBEKANNTER Pumm, pumm: schau nur hinein, schau! *(Zwingt sie, in den Koffer hineinzuschauen)*
LILA Nein, lass mich in Ruhe, ich bin nicht böse, ich bin kein Ungeheuer! Bestiaccia!
UNBEKANNTER Bleib so, es ist schön! Bleib so, es ist schön! *(lacht)*

Der Unbekannter holt aus dem Koffer ein komplette Sexshopmusterkollektion, zieht sich einige Stücke an, zwingt Lila, sie anzufassen usw. In der Zwischenzeit steigt aus der Kaffeemaschine ein dichter Dampf, in dem die Szene langsam verschwindet.

UNBEKANNTER Die Psyche ist eine Dampfmaschine: wenn alle Ventile verstopft sind, besteht das Risiko, dass sie früher oder später kaputtgeht. Und du bist kaputtgegangen!
LILA Das ist nicht wahr!

UNBEKANNTER Ach, ein? Und dieser Phallus aus weichem Gummi … hast du davon nicht heute Nacht geträumt, als du unter der Bettdecke das Übliche tatest?
LILA Schluss, ich bitte dich!
(Singt eintönig vor sich hin, während die ganze Bühne sich mit Dampf verhüllt).

Der Traum meiner bösen
Gedanken kennt die Qual,
die mich im tiefsten bedrängt.
Wenn ich allein bleibe,
habe ich Angst vor
meiner dunkeln Seite.

Schnelle Blitzlichter, die Baphomet und seine Erscheinung als Ungeheuer beleuchten. Dann, unter Lilas verzweifelten Schreien und seinem Gelächter, wird es dunkel.

OFFENER BRIEF AN EIN BELIEBIGES UNGEHEUER

Lila liest:
Liebes Ungeheuer,
unsägliches Leid, massloser Schmerz erfüllen mich, und um mich herum ist nichts als qualvolles Schweigen. Noch immer warte ich auf das Zeichen, das mir deine Hilferufe trotz allem zu versprechen schienen, um mit dir in Verbindung zu treten.
Ich frage mich, wie du es aushältst, mit den Gespenstern deiner grausamen Vergangenheit zu leben, mit dem Schuldgefühl, das dich ganz sicher verfolgt. Ich frage mich, ob und wie du die Ängste und Qualen überwindest, die dich zweifellos bedrängen, denn Reste von Menschlichkeit habe ich auch in dir entdecken können. Du hast mich in meinem Innersten verletzt, meine aufrichtigste Liebe mit Füssen getreten, und ich frage mich ohne Unterlass: warum?
In einem Alptraum ohne Ende frage ich mich immer wieder: "Wie sehr hat er gelitten"? Versuche mich zu erinnern: "Was hat er gesagt? Was hat er geschrien? Was hat er gebrüllt?", als du ihn gefoltert hast? Und als deine Augen ihn trafen, wie war da sein Blick? … vorwurfsvoll, entsetzt, bestürzt? Oder einfach überrascht über so vien unerwartete Grausamkeit? Sag es mir, irgendwie, und sag mir auch, was du empfindest, was du fühlst, wie due weiterleben kannst, als sei nichts gewesen, wie du weiter unter die Leute gehen kannst, zu Freunden, wie due weiter arbeiten kannst, dich weiter vergnügen kannst mit der Erinnerung an eine solche Untat, mit dem

Bild des armen Opfers vor Augen, das du so töricht deinen egoistischen Trieben geopfert hast?

Ich möchte dir in die Augen sehen und versuchen zu verstehen ja, verstehen!, was du jetzt empfindest, ob du das Bedürfnis hast, dich von dieser Tat, die dein Leben zeichnet, zu befreien, ob die Bedeutung deines Scheiterns in der Intimität, der Zwecklosigkeit Deines Handelns dich quälen, so wie mich die Wirklichkeit des Todes heimsucht.

Hilf mir wenigstens, zu begreifen, lass mich fühlen, dass es nicht wahr ist, dass du ein "Ungeheuer" bist. Du bist nur ein einsamer Mensch, der trotz des Bösen, das er tut, und auch aus anderen Gründen, gemeinsam mit mir leidet: weil wir in unserer Menschlichkeit beleidigt worden sind.

Versuche, so zu handeln, dass das Schweigen nicht zur Zerstörung jeglichen Gefühls führt.

Ein Ungeheuer namens LILA

KURZER AUFTRITT BAPHOMETS

(angezogen wie ein Show-Master, führt er ein paar lächerliche Zauberkunststücke vor, dazu Jahrmarktsmusik)

Rate mal, rate mal.
was ist dieses, was ist jenes?
Spitz die Ohren,
auch wenn es dir lächerlich erscheint,
oft Gehörtes noch einmal zu hören.

Also …

Mal ist es ein Gegeimnis, das der menschliche Gesit zu verstehen glaubt, doch dem Frevler bleibt sein Sinn vorenthalten, und wenn er es auf der Suche nach sich selbst zu fassen glaubt, rieselt es ihm durch die Finger wie Sand.

Was ist das? Was ist das?
Was ist das?
Drei Sekunden Zeit
gibt's für die Antwort
oder zur Hölle steigst
du mit mir herab.

Eins, zwei … drei?

Wie bitte? Lächerlich!
Ihr habt es nicht erraten?
Es ist das Unendliche!

Na gut, na gut, na gut!
Versuchen wir es noch einmal.

Was ist das für ein Ding,
das da ist, wenn es weg ist?

Wieder nichts? Das kann doch nicht wahr sein?
Habt ihr's wirklich nicht erraten? Na, der Finger von einem Papagallo, der
im Bus einer Frau an den Hintern fasst.

Na gut, na gut, na gut?
Zwei zu Nulla für mich.

Ich hol euch später ab,
wenn ich mit meinem Spiel zuende bin,
erst gehe ich einen Kaffee trinken.

(geht)

*Die Szene wird zum Inneren einer Gefängniszelle. Das Fenster im Hintergrund ist
geblieben, aber mit schweren Gitter versehen. Es ist Nacht: durch das Fenster sieht man
einen übertrieben riesigen Mond, der fast lebendig wirkt. Lila sitzt auf einer Pritsche, an
die Wand gelehnt, die Knie angezogen, die Arme darumgeschlungen, der Blick ist starr.
Sie singt.*

LILA

Die Leere meiner bösen
Gedanken kennt jede Qual,
die mich im tiefsten bedrängt.
Wenn ich allein bleibe,
habe ich Angst
vor meiner dunklen Seite.

*Pötzlich beginnt der Mond sich zu verwandeln. Er wird rot, ihm wachsen Hörner und –
durch eine Dia-Projektion von hinten, wird er zu Baphomet: dem Teufel.*

BAPHOMET-MOND Hallo, LILA!
LILA Hallo, Mond!
BAPHOMET-MOND Wie geht's dir?
LILA Wie immer. Schlecht. Ich bin so deprimiert.
BAPHOMET-MOND Ich seh's. Aber warum nur, das Leben ist doch
schön!
LILA Ich bin böse. Für mich ist das Leben nicht schön. Ein Alptraum.

BAPHOMET-MOND Las dich nicht so hängen! Würdest du gern da rauskommen? Wir könnten auf den Jahrmarkt gehen … in die Gesiterbahn, zum Beispiel. Das wäre doch toll! Das wäre ein Spass!
LILA Nein. Du willst nur, dass ich noch mehr leide.
BAPHOMET-MOND Aber nein, ich möchte dir helfen, dich auf andere Gedanken bringen, glaub mir, eine Erklärung suchen, eine Lösung, einen Ausweg, ich möchte deine höllischen Schmerzen lindern …
LILA Habt Mitleid! Helft mir, ich will nicht noch einmal von vorne anfangen, ich will nicht wieder Böses tun, behaltet mich hier drin und schliesst fest ab … und dann werft den Schlüssel weg. Und du, geh weg, du Untier! Gettverdammtes!
BAPHOMET-MOND Wenn due nicht zu mir kommst, dann komm ich eben zu dir. Bis bald! So einfach kommt man nicht von sich los, von dem Dämon in uns, und solange man lebt, wird man die Grenzen des Gewissens versuchen auszuweiten. Lila, bis bald! Das ist das Schicksal …

Der Mond kehrt zu seiner ursprünglichen Gestalt zurück. Ganz plötzlich steht Lila auf, geht zum Spiegel und zieht Grimassen, sie kneift sich und gibt sich Ohrfeigen.

LILA Wer bist du, he? Wer bist du? Ungeheuer? Oder Person? Tier oder Mensch? Verstehst du? Hörst du mich? Hörst du mich? *(ohrfeigt sich hysterisch)* Ich rede mit dir, mein Kind! *(mit Kinderstimme)* Mama, Mama, was ist das Rote da, Blut? *(mit Erwachsenenstimme)* Wie oft habe ich dir schon gesagt, dass du dich da nicht anfassen sollst! Fass dich dort nie wieder an, anfassen ist schlecht, das ist der Satan! *(geht aufs Bett zurück und weint)*

Es werden Schritte laut. Jemand hantiert mit einem dicken Schlüsselbund. Wie in einem Alptraum schnappt das Schloss nach zahlreichen Drehungen des Schlüssels auf. Das Quetschen der Türangel beim Öffnen der Tür ist extrem laut, fast so, dass es wehtut (jedes Geräusch muss verstärkt werden, hat eine psychologische Funktion).
Baphomet tritt ein (alias der Unbekannte, mit der Maske des Teufels).

UNBEKANNTER Guten Abend, mein Fräulein.
LILA Du?
UNBEKANNTER Zu deinem Unglück, aber auch ein wenig zu meinem, bin ich in Deinen Hirnmechanismen gefangen. Ich möchte so gern heraus, einen kleinen Spaziergang machen, etwas frische Luft schnappen, statt andauernd diese übelriechende stinkende Luft dieser Kloake einzuatmen, aber ich kann nicht: ich bin dein Gefangener.
LILA Nein, ich bin deine Gefangene.
UNBEKANNTER Was soll ich dazu sagen? Ich bin Dein Geschöpf und damit basta. Das ist die Wahrheit. Ob du willst oder nicht!

LILA Beweise es mir doch.

UNBEKANNTER Ich existiere nur, wenn du mich denkst. Wenn ich aus deinen Gedanken verschwinde, bin ich weg. Es hängt alles nur von dir ab, Lila, auch das Böse, das durch mich repräsentiert wird. Gegen meinen Willen. Satan existiert, das ja, aber im Menschen, der sein Schöpfer ist. Und du hast mich aus dem Nichts geschaffen: du Mörderin! Schau mich doch an, wie hässlich ich bin, monströs, widerlich: aber du hast mich nach deinem Ebenbild geform, du Ungeheuer!

Sie singt ihr Klagelied und hält sich dabei die Ohren zu.

LILA

Die Last meiner bösen
Gedanken kennt die Qual,
die mich im tiefsten bedrängt.
Wenn ich allein bleibe,
habe ich Angst
vor meiner dunklen Seite.

Sie ist wie vom Teufel besessen, von epileptischen Zuckungen befallen.

UNBEKANNTER Es ist Zeit: mit einem Schlag ist ihr Abstieg in ihn Inneres abgeschlossen: die Seele ist an ihrem Ziel im Reich des Dunkeln angelangt. Jetzt, jetzt! Sie ist bereit zum letzten Sprung in ihre Hölle, in der das Unbezähmbare tobt, und endlich kann sie ohne Hindernisse ihre tierischen Anteile ausleben *(zu ihr gewendet)*. Betrachte dich im Spiegel, Lila, jetzt bist du endlich du selbst, jetzt erkenne ich dich.

LILA *(betrachtet sich im Spiegel und sieht, dass sie sich in ein Ungeheuer verwandelt hat)* Neeeiiin!

BAPHOMET *(bringt eine Apparatur für Elektroschocks auf die Bühne. Beim Sprechen schnallt er Lila an und befestig die Kabel an ihrem Kopf und Körper)* Wenn man sich selbst Schaden zufügt, gibt es keine Rettung: weil man sich freiwilling in einer geistigen Hölle einschliesst. Vielleicht muss man von der Krankheit geheilt werden, Mensch zu sein. Man müsste schon bei der Geburt verdammt sein, nur für die Schuld, geboren zu sein! Glücklich diejenigen, die nie das Licht der Welt erblickt haben, die nicht sind, die nicht waren und die nicht sein werden: sie werden keine schmerzlichen Erinnerungen, keine Enttäuschungen und keine Ängste haben. Nichts! Eine unerreichbare Ruhe! Unerschütterlich über den Dingen stehen. In jenem Nichts gibt es weder Gott, noch Sünde, nur unermesslich viel nie gelebte Zeit. Abstrakt, unbekannt, sinnentleert. Verstehst du? Nein? Macht nichts. Steigen wir hinab, Lila, immer weiter hinunter, ins Dunkel deines

Bewusstseins: wir sind schon fast am Boden angelangt, dort, we das helle Licht der Vernunft sich im Schein eines dunklen Lichtes verliert, in der Nacht aller Zeiten. Hier verlierst du jegliche Ahnung von dir selbst … *(einschmeichelnd, seine Stimme entfernt sich immer mehr und es wird allmählich dunkler)* Adieu, Lila, adieu … *(Er verpasst ihr einen Stromstoss, Lila zuckt zusammen. Als er die Voltzahl verdoppelt, wird Lila stocksteif wie eine zum Tode Verurteilte auf dem eklektrischen Stuhl).*
(Dunkel)

LETZTER AUFTRITT BAPHOMETS
(Epilog)

Baphomet, auf dem Thron der Unterwelt, liest in einem alten Buch, während Lila, inzwischen zur Teufelin geworden, zu seinen Füssen obszöne Dinge treibt.

BAPHOMET *(liest) Mehr als allen anderen wäre der Mensch, der sich ja als Meisterwerk Gottes betrachtet, in der Lage, den Beweis für die Unfähigkeit und Arglist des angeblichen Schöpfers anzutreten. In diesem sensiblen, intelligenten, denkenden Wesen, das sich für den Gegenstand der göttlichen Auserwählung hält, und das sich Gott wie sein Ebenbild vorstellt, sehen wir nichts als eine schwächliche, defekte, anfällige Maschine. Wäre es nicht also besser, eine Maschine ohne Seele zu sein, statt ein abergläubischer Unruhegeist, der unter dem Joch seines Gottes und angesichts der unendlichen Qualen, die ihn in seinem zukünftigen Leben erwarten zittert?*
Was meinst du dazu, Lila? Hat der gute alte Spinoza recht?
Gibt es ein zukünftiges Leben? Gibt es eine Hoffnunf für den Menschen?
Un wenn ja, welche?
LILA Miauuu!
BAPHOMET Gut, Lila. Du hast wirklich alles verstanden! Besser als Spinoza!
LILA Miauuu!
BAPHOMET Wau, wau!

Sie umklammern sich, küssen sich. Sie sind jetzt nur noch von einem Punkrtreflektor beleuchtet. Baphomet hebt den Blick, und mit verlegenem Lächeln zwinkert er dem Publikum zu. Dann drückt er auf einen Knopf und küsst Lila erneut.
Auf die beiden fällt ein kleiner Vorhang mit den Worten.

DUNKEL

Auf den Bühnenhintergrund werden Bilder von Ungeheuern aller Art und Dimensionen projiziert.

UN MONSTRE NOMME' LILA

d'Enrico Bernard

Texte français Gérard Cherqui et Silvia Contarini

Personnages

LILA
L'INCONNU (Baphomet)

INCIPIT

Vous qui vous aventurez dans cette représentation
N'espérez pas en sortir joyeux ou rassurés
Abandonnez toute espérance, vous qui entrez!

Quand un cri vous laissera ébahis et médusés;
abasourdis, vous vous demanderez: est-ce moi qui ait crié?
Ou quelqu'un s'en prend-il à moi?

En vérité, pour connaître l'enfer, il suffit de regarder
En nous-mêmes: nous sommes tous des monstres imparfaits, à
differents degrés.

Pour vaincre le Mal,
Il faut le débusquer là où il se terre,
dans notre égoîsme et pas ailleurs. Il nous est inconcevable
que la bête qui nous bouleverse et nous effraie,
soit l'œuvre d'un être anormal, étranger, d'un monstre, précisément!
Venu du néant et retourné au néant
Après une pénible vie terrestre
En marge de la soi-disant normalité.
Nos, mesdames et messieurs, le Mal, le Monstre,
C'est nous!
Il n'est pas aisé de s'en défaire, il nous faut pour cela

Avoir le courage de pratiquer une operation chirurgicale sur nous-
mêmes.
Nous naissons avec des instincts, avec un gout de sang dans la bouche,
Et le cordon ombilical coupé (et combine fait moins souffrir
Mourir que naître!). Le demon de la vie
Se déchaîne alors et s'empare de nous! Et seules
L'évolution des consciences, l'éducation, la culture
Parviennent enfin – et avec quel mal, et pas toujours, et pas entièrement
–
À traquer ce démon. Mais le chemin est plein d'obstacles,
De pièges, il est obscur, il est ardu: qui se perd
En route vers lui-même, à la rencontre de notre "ami"
Le monstre, celui-là risque de connaître le sort
Du protagoniste de cette pièce qui va commencer.

Décor

*L'intérieur d'une auberge de montagne située à la frontière entre les
régions de langue italienne et celles de langue allemande. Il porrai
s'agir du Sud-Tirol ou du Tessin, de nos jours. Il est 5 heures. Un matin
très froid matin d'hiver. Il fait encore nuit et dans la pénombre de la
salle on entend le sifflement du vent et le bruissement de la forêt. Les
ombres des arbres, sur la fenêtre du fond, sont comme des âmes
inquiètes, impuissantes à s'élever vers ciel.*
*On entend l'appel d'un lout solitaire. Tour à coup, dans un coin sombre
de la pièce, il se passe un phénomène paranormal: deux grands yeux
rouge-sang de bête s'allument. Éclate un rire démoniaque. Dans le
silence, on entend une vibration de plus en plus profonde. Un cœur, le
cœur de Lila, bat avec fureur. Un cri.*
*Lila entre. Elle est déjà habillée mais doit encore se coiffer et remonter
ses bas. Elle exécutera ces opérations avec des gestes ambigues, que
l'on porrai interpréter comme des formes sournoises d'auto-érotisme.*

LILA Quelle nuit! Je n'ai pas fermé l'œil. J'avais l'impression que le
vent pouvait passer à travers les pores des murs, en pénétrer les parois.
Et moi, blottie dans un coin de mon lit, enveloppée dans les couvertures,
la tête enfouie dans l'oreiller, j'avais des sueurs froides et je tremblais
en entendant ces voix déformées; quells sons horrible: des courants
d'air infernaux provenant de visions de … de … (rien que d'y penser,
ce me dégoûte) de cadavres démembrés, amoncelés dans mon esprit
tourmenté, si bien que j'en perdais le sommeil.

Le spectre de mes pensées
Toutes de noir-foncé
Connaît bien les tourments
Qui m'agitent en dedans.
Je suis seule et j'ai peur,
Ma part d'ombre me rend pleine de frayeur.

Un cauchemar, sait-on jamais pourquoi! … J'étais moi, mais dédoublée, je m'approchais du lit où j'étais sans defense, victim et bourreau à la fois. Et cette lame que j'empoignais, que je plongeais en moi reflétait des lueurs sinistres … Les mots que j'entendais sortir de ma bouche … je ne peux pas les répéter, mais ce n'était pas moi qui parlais, c'était un autre moi que je ne connaissais pas et qui … *(elle cache sa tête entre ses mains)* Oh! Heureusement la nuit est passée, ou presque! L'été, à cette heure-ci, on entend déjà le chant des oiseaux …! L'obscurité, telle une chrysalide, enveloppe le jour naissant déjà éteint … *(surprise par ses mots)* J'ai dit ça? Comment ai-je pu, moi, une simple villageoise timide … Et pourtant, tant que dure la nuit, je parle comme un poète inspiré par son démon … Démon? Mais alors ce serait le démon qui parle en moi, avec moi! Comme une petite voix soufflant sa réplique à celui qui, ensuite, la répète. Voilà ce que c'est que ce vent! C'est ce diable qui fait trembler les pins, les branches sèches et gelée des hêtres, pour qu'ils nomment les choses, les pensées qu'un autre sème en moi comme du sperme … Qu'ai-je dit, mon Dieu, qu'ai-je dit *(elle se signe)* Mon esprit vagabonde dans le noir comme un aveugle à la lumière du soleil. Affreux est cet irréel engendré par la pénombre, où les objets s'évanouissent pour revenir sous des formes changées: l'ombre du dossier de chaise se fait ricanement stanique de la table; la lampe vacillante, chauve-souris en laquelle il se transfigure, Lui, le Seigneur des Ténèbres qui est en nous, des Ténèbres qu'il éclaire, Lui, de sa lumière spectrale. Lucifer est son nom, le porteur de lumière. Précisément. Et quelle lumière!

Le cygne de mes pensées
Toutes de noir-foncé
Connaît bien les tourments
Qui m'agitent en dedans.
Je suis seule et j'ai peur,
Ma part d'ombre me rend pleine de frayeur.

Du calme, Lila, du calme. Ce n'est pas de ta faute si on n'est pas en été et si le phallus du jour n'a as encore pointé … Pourquoi ai-je dit "phallus"? Comment je parle? Avec les mots de Satan, sans doute. Tais-toi, tais-toi, ma bouche! Ne dis pas des choses que tu ne sais pas, que tu ne peux pas savoir. Et si je te dis que tu ne peux pas savoir, tu dois me croire! *(pause)* C'est bien, Lila, à présent détends-toi et pense que bientôt la fenêtre se remplira de lumière, la lumière baignera la pièce et pénétrera dans tes yeux et dans ton esprit, en le fécondant … La lumière? Sans doute sa lumière à lui, à Lucifer, qui veut me pénétrer et me féconder! Et je ne peux pas lui dire Vade retro! Car je me suis possédée moi-même, en m'ouvrant à lui, ce cochon, ce porc, et je me suis salie de ses excréments, de son urine, de cette salive fétide qu'il a laissée sur les bouts de mes seins, sur mes lèvres … partout, comme un souvenir, un avertissement infernal disant: tu es faite de chair! Mais la chair, Lila, se fane, et le Père sait que tu as péché, il a vu, il a entendu …

Assez, Lila, ça suffit maintenant. Tu as trop parlé par sa voix, trop nombreux sont les mots du mal glissant sur tes lèvres humides, sur lesquelles un jour tu as mis du rouge pour te déguiser en femme … *(désespérée)* Maman, pourquoi tu me frappes? *(voix d'adulte)* Tu as gâché mon rouge à lèvres, regarde, il est bon à jeter! Tu joues déjà à la petite salope, à ton âge! *(elle redevient enfant)* Et lui, au lieu de me consoler, m'emporter avec lui, me prendre dans ses bras, il me punit, dit que c'est mal, mal, d'être femme et enfant à la fois! Méchante! Sale petite méchante. *(pleure)*

Ne pleure plus, tu es grande à présent, il n'y a que dans tes rêves que tu peux redevenir ce que tu étais. Les rêves sont si irréels, ils ne méritent pas qu'on y croit! À qui servent-ils? Bah, à nous-mêmes peut-être, pour nous faire souffrir, ou bien à ce mal qui est en nous et qui doit bien sortir quelque part … eh! Qu'est-ce que je connais des rêves, moi! Pourquoi suis-je la à me tourmenter? J'ai du travail, il faut que je range avant d'ouvrir … *(encore attire par le discours qu'elle suivait)* Les rêves ne sont que des lieux d'incertitude où la raison est comme une coquille vide, un crâne mort … Ah! Quelle idée! Arrête-toi, ma pauvre petite tête, avant qu'il ne soit trop tard … *(d'une voix enfantine)* Maman, j'ai fait un mauvais rêve, j'ai rêvé que papa m'offrait un gros champignon venimeux … *(redevient normale)* Les brioches ne sont pas encore arrivées, il faudra réchauffer celles d'hier, de toute façon, personne ne s'en apercevra, avec leurs bouches pâteuses, pleines de sommeil … J'ai fait un drôle de rêve, que je ne m'explique pas: c'était comme si les objets n'avaient pas de consistence et que je flottais tout autour; ils n'opposaient aucune résistance à mon corps, donc il n'était pas là, mais j'y plongeais quand même comme s'ils étaient dépourvus de matière. Même mes couvertures me paraissaient des vagues me submergeant, noyant mon soufflé, ma réalité, dans le vide. Un immense ocean s'agitait en moi m'entraînant dans un gouffre infini. Et au fond de cet abîme, la bête écarquillait ses yeux de braise … Ah, c'est horrible! *(elle cache sa tête entre ses mains)*

Derrière Lila, qui n'aperçoit pas encore sa presence, apparaît L'Inconnu. Il boite légèrement, est habillé d'un pardessus anonyme et d'un chapeau noir aux bords amples. Il porte une valise.

INCONNU Certains mauvais rêves, mademoiselle, mieux vaut, parfois, les abandonner aux monsters.

LILA *(étonnée)* Qui êtes-vous?

INCONNU Je voudrais juste prendre un petit déjeuner, si cela était possible.

LILA Je ne vous ai pas entendu entrer.

INCONNU Oui, je sais, je suis entré doucement exprès. Je ne voulais pas déranger votre, comment dois-je l'appeler, votre … soliloque.

LILA Dites plutôt mon délire.

INCONNU N'exagérez pas. Tour au plus s'agit-il d'un monologue intérieur asses anodin. Rassurez-vour, il n'y a là rien d'important; ce n'est ni grave ni compromettant. Croyez-moi. Un petit état d'altération mentale passagère due à la pleine lune, qui sait, ou bien à une surexcitation provoquée par la chaleur des couvertures, ce qui invite parfoir l'esprit à ramener le corps à une simple chose dominée exclusivement par le PP, c'est-à-dire, le Principe du Plaisir: l'instinct primaire de l'être humain. En langue allemande, vous appelez ça Lustprinzip.

LILA Je ne sais … mais … je rêve? *(incertaine)* Vous êtes bien là, n'est-ce pas? Je veux dire: vous êtes reel … ou dois-je me pincer? Il y a un instant je vous ai cru transparent, comme traversé de lumière … une étrange lumière … une lumière surnaturelle …

INCONNU Transparent, moi? Peut-être. Après tout, je n'ai pas mangé depuis hier soir.

LILA Pourtant, excusez-moi d'insister, mais vous semblez fait d'air … créé par un tourbillon de ce vent qui siffle à travers les fissures de la fenêtre, à travers les fentes, les interstices. Vous êtes sûr de ne pas être …?

INCONNU Eh, eh! C'est drôle! Vous me prenez pour un fantôme? Non, navré de vous décevoir, je n'appartiens à votre rêve, ou à votre cauchemar, si vous préférez (bien que … vous m'ayez l'air de pouvoir rêver les yeux ouverts). Non, je ne suis pas cette "bête" que vous avez pu apercevoir en vous penchant au-dessus du gouffre … c'est bien cela, non? Écoutez, je vous répète: je ne suis qu'un client. Peut-être le premier, à cette heure, mais il faut bien commencer par quelqu'un. Alors, moi ou un autre … Ou êtes-vous encore fermé?

LILA C'est bientôt ouvert.

INCONNU Ce n'est pas une réponse sérieuse. Vous essayez de ménager la chèvre et le chou; c'est ouvert ou fermé? Dites-le clairement, ou je m'en vais.

LILA Je finis de me coiffer et je cuis à vous.

INCONNU Quel dommage, il me faudra repartir. Je crois d'ailleurs que je me suis trompé de route, je me suis beaucoup éloigné. Quand j'ai vu que la route goudronnée finissait et qu'il y avait la forêt, je me suis dit: sale monde, il va m'arriver le même truc qu'au père Dante, à cause de la forêt obscure, vous savez? J'ai tourné, et encore tourné, et puis j'ai vu votre enseigne allumée. J'ai arêté la voiture et je me suis dit: c'est une région de chasseurs, possible qu'ils sont ouverts. Je suis descendu de la voiture et je me suis dit …

LILA Oui, une fois descendu, vous vous êtes dit?

INCONNU Vous vous moquez de moi, je vous comprends. Quand on s'égare comme un imbécile … J'ai quitté l'autoroute parce que à force d'avancer tout droit j'ai cru devenir fou … vous savez, j'ai conduit toute la nuit. Alors, j'ai pris la nationale, histoire de me réveiller avec quelques virages, ensuite cette petite départementale toute en lacets, et ainsi de suite, jusqu'à cette espèce de chemin escarpé …

LILA Vous avez de la chance, il y a peu de temps qu'il a été goudronné. Il était question d'abattre la forêt et de raccorder à l'autoroute. Mais les écologistes n'étaient pas d'accord et le projet est tombé à l'eau. Dommage, ç'aurait pu être une bonne affaire pour le village.

INCONNU Alors, j'aurais trouvé, en pleine forêt, au lieu d'une auberge, une station service 24 heures sur 24.

LILA Avec buffet self service.

INCONNU Pour camionneurs.

LILA C'est toujours mieux que les chasseurs … ils se croient supérieurs parce qu'ils portent un fusil.

INCONNU Mauvais signe, votre aversion du fusil. Cela signifie que vous n'avez pas surmonté le complexe d'électre ou, comme dit le grand Sigmund, que vous éprouvez encore l'envie du pénis.

LILA Je n'y comprends rien. Je ne connais pas votre Sigmund et je trouve stupide cette façon de parler. Et, si vous le permettez, arrogante envers moi. Vous prenez des libertés avec moi parce que vous savez que j'ai honte de vous répondre comme vous le méritez. Alors, s'il vous plait, cessez de m'importuner avec vous doubles sens car je vois bien où vous voulez en venir.

INCONNU Franchement, mademoiselle, vos frustrations sexuelles ne me concernent pas. Je veux juste un café et savoir comment sortir de cette ... cette forêt obscure, puisque il faut bien l'appeler ainsi.

LILA Pour le café, il faudra patienter quelques minutes, la machine n'est pas encore sous tension.

INCONNU *(résigné)* J'attends.

LILA Asseyez-vous.

INCONNU Vous plaisantez? Je suis resté assis toute la nuit. Je vais me dégourdir un peu le jambes, sinon je ne pourrais jamais me taper un kilometer de plus.

LILA Pourquoi, vous allez où? Au bout du monde?

INCONNU Pourquoi pas? Au fond, c'est partout pareil.

LILA Vous allez au sud?

INCONNU Oui, je vais en enfer, avec votre permission.

LILA Ne vous fâchez pas. Nous autres, ici, on a nos habitudes, le village est petit, tout le monde se connaît, il n'y a pas de secrets ... et puis, vous être libre d'aller où vous voulez, même au sud. Il doit bien y avoir des braves gens, la bas aussi, comme vous et moi. Vous me pardonnez?

INCONNU C'est moi qui vous demande pardon. La fatigue me fait dire des bêtises. Je ne suis pas comme ça d'ordinaire, je vous assure.

LILA C'est ma faute, je ne suis pas capable de rester à ma place ... Et puis il est grand temps d'en finir, avec toutes ces histories de sud et de nord, comme s'il n'y avait pas d'est et ouest. *(change)* Vous savez, j'ai eu aussi une nuit agitée ... il fait encore nuit?

INCONNU Ni nuit, ni jour ... ce moment indéfini où les créatures de l'obscurité – celles des rêves – reviennent rapidement à leur lieu d'origine, alors que la lumière du soleil n'a pas encore dissipé les ténèbres.

LILA Vouz parlez obscurément ... pourtant je vous comprends, ou crois vous comprendre ... Bizarre!

INCONNU Cela vous étonne?

LILA Cela ne devrait pas?

INCONNU On dit que c'est l'heure des âmes en peine ...

LILA Comme la mienne!

INCONNU Des âmes qui ne sont pas descendues à l'enfer, mais qui n'ont pas encore trouvé le paradis. C'est un purgatoire où se baladent des mostre qui n'ont jamais eu le courage de s'épanouir dans toute leur animalité, des mostre inachevés, esquissés, des mostre insensés, ou, tout au plus, le fruit de fantasmes inconséquents, des feux follets de l'esprit qui s'allume pour se réchauffer lui-même dans son abstraction dramatique, dans son isolation mentale tragique et, excusez-moi, un peu masturbatoire! C'est de la branlette d'esprit qui croit s'éclairer, tout comme une ampoule qui s'imagine qu'elle reflète les rayons du soleil. Alors, à quoi bon faire vagabonder ses propres pensées monstrueuses dans ce purgatoire où tout n'est que buée, apparence sans contenu?

LILA Excusez-moi, mais j'ai bien peur de ne pas vous suivre.

INCONNU Je disais: pourquoi penser de manière abstraite à ce monstre qui est en nous au lieu de … de… vous voyez …

LILA Je ne vois pas et je ne veux pas le voir.

INCONNU Ou bien vous avez peur?

LILA Et même si cela était?

INCONNU Ce n'est pas si dur. Laissez-vous aller.

LILA Des craintes, des craintes vacue. Vous l'avez dit: abstraites.

INCONNU *(rassurant)* Vous verrez: aux premières lueurs de l'aube vos peurs ancestrales (et un peu puerile, je regretted) s'évanouiront. Et dans le calice transparent de la vie (pardonnez mon emphase, mais il faut ce qu'il faut) ne coulera plus le sang, mais une lymphe verte, vitale, comme les feuilles et les pousses du printemps. Êtes-vous rassurée?

LILA Allez, ouste! J'ai du travail!

INCONNU Vous avez tort de faire confliance au jour qui va naître et qui n'est pas encore là. Un soleil qui n'est pas levé c'est comme des intérêts bancarie qui n'ont pas donné.

LILA Vous êtes un beau parleur.

INCONNU C'est vrai. Le jour favorise la pensée rationnelle, lucide, alors que les ténèbres libèrent dans l'esprit … laissons tomber, après tout vous avez raison, c'est trop gênant *(silence)* Vous avez de jolies jambes, vous savez?

LILA Moi? Elles sont tordues.

INCONNU Des jambes d'amazone. Vous montez à cheval?

LILA Je monte, oui, à moto.

INCONNU Vous êtes une sportive.

LILA Quand j'ai des idées noires, je mets mon casque et je pars, sans même savoir où, et je tourne, je tourne en rond comme une idiote. Cela m'arrive souvent …

INCONNU Quel genre d'idées? Sexuelles, n'est-ce pas?

LILA *(fâchée)* S'il vous plait!

INCONNU Je vous en prie, vous êtes libre de ne pas en parler.

LILA Il ne manquerait plus que ça …

INCONNU Moi, si j'étais vous, j'en parlerais.

LILA Et pourquoi donc?

INCONNU Trop de tension, la machine pourrait exploser.

LILA Qu'est-ce qui vous fait croire que la tension est trop forte?

INCONNU Ça se voit.

LILA Vraiment? À quoi?

INCONNU A la vapeur. Vous ne pouvez pas voir, mais moi si: la machine à café derrière vous, elle est sur le point d'exploser. Vous devriez vous dépêcher avant que ce soit trop tard! Bordel, je vous dis que ça va péter! Faites quelque chose! *(en effet, une dense vapeur se dégage du comptoir).*

LILA Oui, oui … *(enragée, en maniant la machine)* Du Hexe!

INCONNU Femmes et moteurs, joies et douleurs!

LILA Ne soyez pas si nul.

INCONNU Je passe le temps: j'ai une faim de loup. Si je ne prends pas tout de suite un café je vais hurler. Vous voulez voir? Ouuuuuuh!

LILA Il va falloir attendre, monsieur le loup! *(en aparté)* On dirait un vrai!

INCONNU Encore! Quelle torture!

LILA J'ai vidé la machine parce que parfois la soupape se coince et ne vidange plus. Elle va se remettre sous tension … soyez patient.

INCONNU De client à patient. Quel accueil! Service compris.

LILA En attendant, je dresse les tables pour le petit déjeuner. Pourquoi ne pas m'aider au lieu de traîner dans mes pattes?

INCONNU Ah non, il n'en est pas question!

LILA Fainéant.

INCONNU Et pourquoi devrais-je vous aider?

LILA Pour me faire gagner du temps.

INCONNU Qu'est-ce que je gagne si je vous aide?

LILA Votre café. Vous désirez autre chose? Une brioche?

INCONNU Je m'en remets à votre bonté.

LILA D'accord. Je vous l'offre, aussitôt qu'elles arrivent.

INCONNU Et si elles n'arrivent pas?

LILA Pourquoi ne devraient-elles pas arriver?

INCONNU A cause la psychose … la psychose du monstre.

LILA Quel monstre? De quoi parlez-vous?

INCONNU Ne faites pas semblant de nepas savoir, je ne suis pas né d'hier.

LILA *(soupçonneuse)* Vous êtes de passage, que savez vous de ce qui se passe dans notre village?

INCONNU On en a parlé dans les journaux … vous ne les lisez pas?

LILA *(vague)* Oui, oui, quand j'ai le temps.

INCONNU Vous n'écoutez pas la radio?

LILA Quand j'ai le temps.

INCONNU Vous ne regardez pas la télé?

LILA *(embêtée)* Quand j'ai le temps.

INCONNU Et quand avez-vous le temps?

LILA Quand vous me laisserez travailler en paix, puisque vous ne voulez pas m'aider.

INCONNU Si c'est pour vous rendre service …

LILA Je parie que c'est la première fois que vous faites le ménage.

INCONNU La première et la dernière fois.

LILA Et qu'en dit votre femme? *(lui donne un plateau avec la vaisselle)*

INCONNU Je ne suis pas marié.

LILA Vous avez alors une fiancée, une petite amie …

INCONNU Non, non. Mieux vaut être seul que mal accompagné.

LILA Je préfère ne plus parler avec vous; vous m'agacez.

Ils commencent à dresser les tables ensemble. Lila chantonne son refrain tandis que l'Inconnu la regarde comme s'il tramait un plan.

LILA Le spectre de mes pensées
Toutes de noir-foncé
Connaît bien les tourments
Qui m'agitent en dedans.
Je suis seule et j'ai peur,
Ma part d'ombre me rend pleine de frayeur.

INCONNU Bravo! Vous chantez comme un ange.

LILA Je ne suis pas un ange.

INCONNU *(ironique)* Pas plus qu'un monstre.

LILA Qui sait …

INCONNU *(plaisantant)* J'ai peur! *(pause)* A propos, vous n'avez pas peur du monstre?

LILA Moi? Pourquoi le devrai-je? Je n'ai fait de mal à personne!

INCONNU Sans doute, mais le monstre, lui, ne fait pas dans le dentelle … Une jolie pouliche comme vous, toute seule … parce que vous tenez cette baraque toute seule, n'est-ce pas?

LILA Nous avions dit: pas de questions!

INCONNU Qui a dit ça?

LILA J'avais cru comprendre … *(comme saisie d'une illumination)* Voià pourquoi depuis quelques jours les chasseurs ont disparus.

INCONNU Ils sont tous partis à la recherché du monstre?

LILA Tu parles. Ce sont trouillards, ils font tous dans leur culotte … Ils se sentent courageux quand ils tirent sur de pauvres alouettes, héroïques quand ils pincent les fesses des filles, mais dès que le monstre est là, ils s'enfuient tête baissée, et c'est encore mieux si c'est chez maman qui garde le seuil rouleau à patisserie à la main. Et on appelle ça des homes! Ils se sont envolés comme leurs oiseaux. *(elle rit, elle a dit une bêtise)*

INCONNU Moi, je suis là. Je ne me suis pas envolé. Ni moi ni mon oiseau *(elle le regarde de travers)* Vous arrêtez de rire? J'ai dit quelque chose de mal? Une allusion de trop, peut-être?

LILA Vous n'êtes pas d'ici, vous êtes de passage. Pourquoi le monstre devrait-it s'en prendre à vous? Vous n'y êtes pour rien.

INCONNU S'il s'agit d'un monstre, il doit bien être un peu fou, non? Et les fous, ma chère, on ne les raisonne pas.

LILA Il est fou, sans doute, pourtant il suit sa propre logique.

INCONNU Qu'en savez-vous?

LILA Intuition féminine.

INCONNU En somme, vous le defendez.

LILA Moi? Non, je vous assure. Je veux seulement dire que les fous ne sont pas toujours des monstres, par fois ils peuvent devenir de grands artistes, comme Cézanne, ou l'autre, celui qui s'est coupé l'oreille.

INCONNU Le fait est que la folie doit être canalisée par un parcours artistique, mais il ne faut pas s'imaginer que l'art est l'apanage de quelques fous qui décident d'être à l'avantgarde du désastre mental de l'homme.

LILA Je ne sais pas! Et je ne saurais dresser … Entschuldingung! Entamer … enfin, bref, parlons d'autre chose, si vous voulez bien.

INCONNU Oui, mais pas de politique, je vous en supplie. Les hommes politiques me font vomir.

LILA Moi aussi. D'accord: ni monstres, ni hommes politiques.

INCONNU Parlons de nous, de nos affaires … dans l'intimité de ce petit matin.

LILA Ne vous faites pas de fausses idées.

INCONNU *(il fait le niais)* Moi?

LILA Oui, vous: où voulez-vous en venir avec vos allusions à peine voilées?

INCONNU Nulle part, je vous assure *(ironique)* je suis un garçon sérieux.

LILA Écoutez: pour moi, vous êtes un monsieur-personne qui s'est arrêté pour prendre un café.

INCONNU Et qui ne l'a pas encore bu. Et de plus on le fouette: au boulot, bosse, esclave! Et la ferme ... Regardez, j'ai déjà préparé deux tables. Vous pouvez dire un mot au patron pour qu'il m'embauche.

LILA C'est moi la patronne.

INCONNU Ah! Cette auberge est à vous ... bien, bien ... un bon parti!

LILA Mes parents sont morts, je n'ai ni famille, ni amis. Je suoi restée seule. Et cela me va. La nuit j'ai bien un peu peur, c'est vrai, mais sinon je ne me débrouille pas trop mal, y compris avec la déclaration des revenus. Je n'ai besoin de personne, pas même d'un comptable!

INCONNU Vous êtes une femme bien, vraiment. Mais ... excusez ma curiosité, vous êtes très jeune ... vos parents? Vous êtes orpheline? Comment est-ce arrivé? Un accident?

LILA Pourquoi? Cela vous intéresse?

INCONNU Laissez-moi devenir: un banal accident de la route dû, sans doute, à la vitesse excessive et à des pneus mal gonflés.

LILA Comment le savez-vous?

INCONNU Simple supposition ... et aussi grâce aux statistiques – la plupart des décès sont dus à la circulation.

LILA *(ironique)* Bravo!

INCONNU Bizarre, quand même, ces pneus dégonflés! Ce n'était pas une distraction de votre cher papa. Il était tatillon, n'est-ce pas, il contrôlait ses pneus à chaque plein d'essence?

LILA Ça suffit. Vous vous mêlez de choses qui ne vous regardent pas.

INCONNU Et vous parents d'adoption? Ils désiraient tellement une petite fille, mais ils ne pouvaient pas en avoir ... là, vous entrez en scène, avec vos tresses, blondes, évidemment. Ne sont-ils pas eux aussi morts dans un malheureux accident? Le gaz ?

LILA Un malheureux accident, oui.

INCONNU Et votre fiancé n'a-t-il pas péri dans un accident de montagne, à trois mille mètres, le jour qui a suivi votre dépucelage? Son pied a glissé? Pardon pour l'image.

LILA *(se révoltant)* Que voulez-vous de moi?

INCONNU Rien, rien, ne vous agitez pas. Je voulais juste dire que vous n'avez pas eu de chance. Trop de malchance, vraiment, trop. Mais malgré les terribles malheurs qui vous ont frappée, malgré les terribles coups dont vous avez été victime, vous vous êtes remise, vous avez géré votre affaire toute seule, au point qu'aujourd'hui nous sommes en présence d'une vraie professionnelle, un véritable chef d'entreprise, un génie du capitalisme. Bravo!

LILA Qui ça, nous?

INCONNU Pluriel de majesté.

LILA Bien, si sa majesté veut bien daigner s'asseoir, je lui prépare son café.

INCONNU Enfin! Et ma bioche?

LILA Une chose à la fois. *(se déplace vers le banc mais bute sur la valise)*

INCONNU Attention!

LILA Scheisse. J'aurais pu me casser le cou. Quelle idée de laisser votre valise dans la pénombre. Je vais la ranger, ici elle gêne.

INCONNU *(brusquement)* N'y touchez pas!

LILA Oh là là, elle est lourde!

INCONNU Doucement, s'il vous plaît, maniez-la avec beaucoup de précaution.

LILA Rien à faire, de vostre valise! Vous n'avez qu'à a déplacer vous même.

INCONNU *(la met sous la table)* Voilà, ici elle ne gêne personne.

LILA Elle est pleine de pierres ou quoi? Elle a l'air de peser une tonne.

INCONNU Des pierres, précisément. Comment avez-vous deviné?

LILA Vous vous moquez de moi?

INCONNU C'est vous qui avez parlé de pierres.

LILA Oui, comme ça.

INCONNU Et si je vous disais que je suis géologue et que dans cette valise j'ai une collection de morceaux de roches, vous me croiriez?

LILA Non.

INCONNU *(il rit)* Et vous auriez raison. Pas de pierres!

LILA Quoi, alors?

INCONNU Du gallium. Vous connaissez? ... Le gallium est un nouvel alliage. Il vient des laboratoires militaires de l'ex Union Soviétique. C'est un supraconducteur d'énergie, je crois.

LILA Et un homme qui transporte un truc si délicat, si mystérieux, va s'égarer dans ces montagnes oubliées de Dieu et du diable?

INCONNU Du diable, non, certainement pas. Il n'oublie jamais rien, ni personne!

LILA Vous êtes un drôle de type.

INCONNU Vraiment? J'ai une tête à claques?

LILA A cette heure-ci, dans la pénombre, une apparition insolite ... vous en conviendrez, on ne vous a jamais vu dans le coin, et si c'était vous ...

INCONNU Le monstre? Pourquoi pas? *(il rit)*

LILA Je ne voulais pas vous froisser.

INCONNU Mais non, je ne suis pas du genre à me vexer facilement, bien au contraire ...

LILA Au contraire, vous y prenez plaisir.

INCONNU C'est ça. J'aimerais avoir votre avis sur ma personne: qui suis-je?

LILA Qu'est-ce que j'en sais, moi?

INCONNU Un monstre, d'accord, mais c'est trop facile.

LILA Dans quel sens?

INCONNU Les étrangers sont tous un peu bizarres, c'est dans l'ordre des choses. Et un monstre est précisément quelqu'un qui n'entre pas dans la régle et se révèle étrange – non? – ambigu, égaré, voire franchement repoussant. C'est bien l'impression que je provoque en vous, peut-être malgré vous?

LILA Je ne sais pas.

INCONNU Oui, à lier. Vous ne me dites pas toute la vérité.

LILA Quelle vérité?

INCONNU Laquelle? Tu ne veux pas t'ouvrir à moi, petite salope? *(il lui saisit un bras, la serre en lui faisant mal. D'un mouvement brusque elle parvient à se libérer)*

LILA Allez vous faire foutre!

INCONNU *(la serrant à nouveau)* J'adore les gros mots, ça m'excite.

LILA Alors, brantez-vous et foutez-moi le paix!

INCONNU Pas encore. Je veux d'abord t'entendre crier ...

LILA Vous me faites mal.

INCONNU Je suis vraiment désolé!

LILA Avec vos ongles si longs vous allez me faire saigner.

INCONNU C'est à cause de ta chair, elle est si tendre, pulpeuse ...

LILA Nom de Dieu! *(au nom de Dieu, il la lâche tout de suite)*

INCONNU Excusez-moi, je plaisantais.

LILA La bonne blague, vous m'avez brisé le bras.

INCONNU Mais non, rien qu'une petite égratignure ... d'accord, je dirai à ma manucure de limer mes griffes.

LILA Dites à votre manucure de vous envoyer au diable de ma part *(en aparté)* quel connard!

INCONNU Comptez sur moi.

LILA Merci. Et ne me touchez plus.

INCONNU Entendu.

LILA Je devrais appeler la police, vous m'avez presque agressée!

INCONNU Presque seulement, presque.

LILA Pourquoi, vous auriez pu aller plus loin? Ces marques sur mon bras ne vous suffisent pas? Regardez, mais regardez donc!

INCONNU Ne vous en faites pas. Ce n'était qu'un moment, un instant de folie. Je sais, j'aurais pu me retenir, je n'aurais pas dû perdre mon sang froid. Mais aussi c'est un peu de votre faute si ...

LILA Ma faute?

INCONNU Votre parfum.

LILA Mais je ne porte aucun parfum.

INCONNU Vous sentez vous-même, vous comprenez?

LILA Non, je préfère ne pas comprendre.

INCONNU Vous sentez la chair ... la chair fraîche!

LILA Bon, à partir de maintenant, gardez vos distances, trois pas minimum. *(elle compte)* Un, deux, trois ... Entendu?

INCONNU Verstanden ... Promis!

LILA Si vous aviez vu comment vous me regardiez! Vos pupilles étaient dilatées et injectées de sang comme ...

INCONNU Une bête?

LILA Exact. Comment ...

INCONNU Comment j'ai deviné?

LILA Oui, vous me faites peur.

INCONNU Enfin!

LILA Ah, et vous trouvez ça amusant? Bon, tant pis pour moi, je n'aurais pas dû me fier au premier venu.

INCONNU Ecoutez, je regrette de vous avois effrayée. Vraiment!

LILA Et vous espérez vous en sortir à si bon compte? Avec des excuses?

INCONNU Pourquoi pas? Après tout il ne s'est rien passé ... rien de vrai, je veux dire.

LILA Et les égratignures? Je les ai rêvées?

INCONNU Assurément non.

LILA Vous voyez? J'ai raison. Il s'est passé des choses graves, des événements incontestables ...

INCONNU Les ongles d'un chat qui ne voulait pas rester dans vos bras, voilà tout.

LILA Et vous seriez ce chat?

INCONNU Pourquoi pas? Le chat me convient.

LILA Et moi la souris, n'est-ce pas?

INCONNU Charmante idée, je n'y avais pas pensé. Heureusement que vous êtes là.

LILA Vous irez en prison.

INCONNU Où sont les témoins? Pour confirmer, affirmer, déposer, etc ...?

LILA Et ma parole?

INCONNU Et l'expertise médicale, gynécologique? Et le test de l'ADN?

LILA J'aurais dû me faire violer pour avoir raison?

INCONNU Dura lex sed lex!

LILA Vous faites le malin, vous savez toujours comment vous sortir de ces situation, vous vous y connaissez en agressions et en arguties juridiques pour éviter les problèmes. Les hommes comme vous devraient être castrés dès l'enfance. Ou noyés, écartelés ... les salauds!

INCONNU Vous exagérez! Vous savez? Ça, c'est la voix du monstre qui est en vous! Faites attention, ne le provoquez pas trop, car s'il devait sortir sa petite tête ... bouh!

LILA Moi, le monstre? Et vous? Qu'êtes-vous? Qu'avez-vous dans votre valise? Les outils du métier, j'en suis sûre! Des poinçons, des chaînes, des crochets de boucher ... Mon Dieu, qu'est-ce que je dis?

INCONNU Pourquoi voulez-vous savoir? Curiosité féminine?

LILA Vous avez quelque chose à cacher?

INCONNU Et si j'avouais que j'ai le cadavre d'une femme découpé en morceaux, que feriez-vous, hein? Vous appelleriez à l'aide?

LILA J'aimerais bien voir!

INCONNU Nous sommes dans un endroit isolé, en lisière de forêt. Le vent emporterait votre voix, qui sait où, qui sait dans quelle gorge déserte ... Pauvre petite, tu me fais de la peine, il faudrait te consoler *(il s'approche d'elle)* à ma façon, naturellement!

LILA *(effrayée)* Vous êtes sérieux?

INCONNU Vérité, imagination, qu'importe! D'ailleurs, c'est bien ce que tu attends de moi!

LILA Moi?

INCONNU Mais oui, vous Madame, précisément: Madame avec son irritante perversité.

LILA Perverse, moi? Toi ... Vous, plutôt.

INCONNU Vous ai-je demandé ce que vous aviez dans votre réfrigérateur? Non, alors vous voyez bien que je ne suis pas pervers. Pour ce que j'en sais, vous et vos antécédents, vous pourriez garder le cadavre d'un bébé à côté de la viande hachée.

LILA La tension monte.

INCONNU La mienne aussi, et comment! C'est de votre faute. Votre férocité inconsciente est très contagieuse.

LILA La tension monte dans la machine à café, mein Gott. Dans cinq minutes je pourrai faire votre maudit café *(drastique)* Und fertig, schluss ! Repartez par où vous êtes venu, dans le néant, dans l'ambigu. D'accord?

INCONNU C'est moi, moi, qui ai hâte de partir.

LILA Cinq minutes, plus que cinq minutes.

INCONNU Une éternité.

LILA Mais non, une broutille.

INCONNU Trois cents secondes, pour être exact.

LILA Et vous appelez ça une éternité?

INCONNU Le temps est une construction subjective. Parfois il passe vite, parfois il semble interminable. En somme, il ne s'écoule pas toujours de la même manière, ni dans la même direction; il avance, il recule, cela dépend. On appelle cela la flèche du temps, car elle suit l'évolution de l'univers, projetée dans le futur ou de retour dans le passé. Par example, la théorie de l'éternel retour ... Nietzsche! Quelle merveille! Un homme un peu survolté, mais avec des couilles ... d'enfer!

LILA Vous m'avez prise pour une sotte? Je suis une villageoise, certes, mais en moi, en dedans, il y a ...

INCONNU Un démon?

LILA *(effrayée)* Le démon?

INCONNU Si vous insistez ...

LILA Non, c'est vous qui insistez trop. Vous avez compris que j'avais peur de vous et vous vous amusez à me torturer. Vous êtes un sadique, un maniaque, un monstre.

INCONNU Parce que mes ongles sont trop longs?

LILA *(menaçante)* Les miens aussi, et je sais me défendre toute seule, ne croyez pas!

INCONNU Certainement, on raconte que le diable est né femme et qu'ensuite il a pris les couilles pour une blague de la nature. Il représente ce qu'on appelle la «femme-queue» ou, comme mon ami Freud l'a appelé, moins vulgairement, la femme phallique. C'est comme si vous, si vous permettez, vous aviez un clitoris des dimensions d'un pénis. Voilà ce qu'est le Seigneur des enfers ou des ténèbres: une queue à l'envers. Le serpent qui se mord la queue ... *(il rit)*

LILA Die listige Schlange ... Vous êtes un serpent maléfique!

INCONNU Oui, Mozart *(chante l'air de la Flûte ...)* Vous croyez au diable?

LILA De nos jours, ce serait ridicule d'y croire.

INCONNU Mais ne pas y croire peut être dangereux ... très dangereux.

LILA A votre avis ... il existe?

INCONNU A mon avis, quelque chose, quelque part, existe. Je ne saurais pas vous dire où ...

LILA Peut- être au centre de la terre ... comme votre métal ... comme s'appelle-t-il déjà?

INCONNU Gallium. Et le gallium n'est pas un métal, c'est un alliage. Et la différence n'est pas petite. Le métal existe dans la nature, l'alliage non, il faut le forger, le créer, il faut soustraire ce qui a été créé pour la récréer autre, comme le diable et l'enfer qui sont des éléments de l'esprit à l'état pur, sauvage, sur lesquels notre imagination parfois brode un peu trop, dépassant les limites, bien au delà de l'humain ... Je vous assomme?

LILA Mein Gott, vous êtes énigmistique.

INCONNU Vous voulez dire énigmatique, fraülein.

LILA Cela s'entend que je suis de langue allemande? Parfois, mon italien est un peu boiteux, je sais.

INCONNU Vous parlez très bien l'italien, mais vous pensez à l'allemande: comme Faust.

LILA Qu'est-ce que cela signifie?

INCONNU Cela signifie que les Allemands ont toujours montré une sympathie morbide et étrange pour le Malin. Avant le Moyen-Age on ne faisait qu'en rire. Je pense à Virgile qui dit ... Les Géorgiques, l'Enéide ... vous avez dû en lire des passages à l'école!

LILA Peut-être ... je n'en suis pas sûre ...

INCONNU Eh bien, à propos de l'Enfer, Virgile dit, plus ou moins, si ma mémoire est bonne: Heureux qui a pu pénétrer les lois de la nature, mettre sous ses pieds les préjugés et les terreurs, le Styx et l'Achéront ... etc. Mais je vous ennuie!

LILA De toute façon, à cette heure, je ne peux plus dormir. Comment conclut votre Virgile?

INCONNU Les portes et le royaume de Pluton, le seuil fatal et le féroce Cerbère, ne sont que des mots vides, des contes pour les enfants, semblables à un rêve importun.

LILA Des contes pour les enfants ... semblables à un rêve importun ... J'avais bien l'impression de vous avoir déjà vu, d'avoir déjà entendu votre voix, comme si votre image et vos mots surgissaient de moi, comme s'ils étaient une projection de mes angoisses, l'incarnation de ce dont j'ai vraiment peur.

INCONNU De quoi avez-vous vraiment peur? Allez, parlez, je n'y tiens plus.

LILA De la mort, peut-être ... Non, plus encore de la souffrance.

INCONNU Et du sexe? De ce «doux dominateur de mon esprit profond, terrible mais très cher don du ciel» dont parle Leopardi?

LILA Je vous ai déjà dit de rester à votre place.

INCONNU   Pardonnez-moi ... mais vous êtes beaucoup trop susceptible. C'est suspect, vous savez!

LILA De la crainte, rien que de la crainte.

INCONNU Oh, vous ne devez pas me craindre, je ne suis pas aussi méchant que j'en ai l'air.

LILA C'est comme si vous connaissiez les aspects les plus obscurs de mon imagination, ceux que j'ignore moi même et qui, parfois, me traînent par les cheveux et me violent avec des images que je préférerais ne pas faire ... Je ne peux m'expliquer mieux.

INCONNU Vous vous expliquez très bien. A des oreilles averties ...

LILA   Je veux dire que votre physionomie n'est pas nouvelle; je reconnais votre voix comme si c'était la mienne *(elle hésite)* C'est drôle ... *(le regarde)* Nous nous sommes déjà rencontrés?

INCONNU   En rêve, peut-être ... Pourquoi pas? *(obscène)* J'adore pénétrer les rêves des jeunes filles! Mmm, un vrai plaisir!

LILA Vous jouez avec le feu.

INCONNU Vous aussi.

LILA *(après une pause de tension)* Alors, ne plaisantons plus avec ces choses-là.

INCONNU Vous avez raison. Les rêves, surtout les cauchemars les nuits de pleine lune sont des espaces dangereux, off limits. Chantier interdit. Vous êtes d'accord? Propriété privée!

LILA *(il rit)* Attention chien méchant.

INCONNU Le chien à trois têtes? Bravo! Comment avez-vous deviné?

LILA *(sans comprendre)* Trois têtes? *(elle plaisante)* Ouah-ouah!

INCONNU *(il joue le jeu)* Oui, c'est ça, ouah-ouah, fait le chien de Pluton posté à l'entrée de l'Enfer. Ouah-ouah!

LILA *(se bloquant)* Ou ... o ...

INCONNU *(sautant autour d'elle à quatre pattes, comme un chien)* Ouah-ouah; ouah-ouah.

LILA *(effrayée)* Assez, vous me faites peur! Arrêtez, ça suffit!

INCONNU Le problème avec les rêves, c'est qu'ils peuvent toujours se réaliser, comme par magie!

LILA Ou par sadisme.

INCONNU Vous m'en voulez?

LILA Non ... Oui ! Vous n'auriez pas dû faire le chien méchant, pas si bien, on aurait dit un vrai chien féroce.

INCONNU Mais non, juste un petit caniche noir.

LILA Vous appelez ça un caniche, vous!

INCONNU Bon, un peu méphistophélique.

LILA S'il vous plaît, ne recommencez pas avec les arcanes ... *(surprise par elle-même)* Drôle de mot ... C'est quoi les arcanes?

INCONNU C'est vous qui l'avez dit.

LILA Oui, c'est moi qui l'ai dit, mais ce n'est pas moi qui l'ai exprimé avec ma pensée ...

INCONNU Tiens! Qui pourrait avoir fait ça ... Pourtant j'ai cru entendre votre voix.

LILA Je suis une fille simple, qu'en sais-je moi de ces termes ... et en italien de surcroît, moi qui suis de langue allemande ... non, je ne peux pas l'avoir pensé.

INCONNU Qui, alors? Le diable?

LILA Vous avez mis ce mot en moi, sur ma langue, vous me l'avez fait dire!

INCONNU Comment ça?

LILA Je ne sais pas. Vous êtes contagieux, vous m'avez attirée dans ce piège dialectique ... voilà, encore un mot qui n'est pas à moi ... et je ne peux plus sortir de ce piège cérébral ... Au secours! Je suis prisonnière d'un monstre.

INCONNU Intérieur ou extérieur? Réel ou imaginaire? Concret ou fantasmagorique? Toucher pour croire ...

LILA Ne me touchez pas!

INCONNU Vous avez vraiment le diable au corps.

LILA Non, je ne joue pas ce jeu-là, votre jeu, espèce de salaud!

INCONNU Bien sûr que vous voulez, vous le voulez ... Ne faites pas la sainte nitouche, comme Marguerite ... *(il la regarde pour l'hypnotiser, le visage de Lila est éclairé d'un reflet étrange)*

LILA Qui est Marguerite?

INCONNU Une vieille copine. Une des nombreuses fiancées que j'ai un peu partout; je suis comme un marin, vous savez, une femme dan chaque port ... Mais la pauvre Marguerite n'est plus là, hélas ... perdue à jamais, morte! Tant pis pour elle ...

LILA *(effrayée)* De quoi est-elle morte?

INCONNU D'une méchante maladie: l'amour! Je veux dire qu'elle a fait l'amour, baisé, copulé, elle s'est faite sauter, bref, elle s'est accouplé charnellement avec un monstre.

LILA Un monstre?

INCONNU Oui, de chair et d'os (peut-être plus d'os que de chair). Un vieillard décrépit déguisé en jeune homme avec une bite longue comme ça *(indique très grand)* et un cœur tout petit comme ça *(indique petit)*. Vous voyez le truc?

LILA Et elle l'aimait? Même s'il était un individu aussi répugnant, aussi odieux?

INCONNU Vous savez, les monstres, ou bien on les aime ou bien on les hait, pas d'alternative. Et totalement, désespérément, jusqu'au plus profond de nous mêmes, jusqu'à la Rédemption du monstre – peu probable, il est vrai – parce que, plus on tombe bas, plus il est difficile de remonter.

LILA Pourquoi me regardez-vous comme ça, comme si vous étiez le monstre?

INCONNU Ne vous inquiétez pas.

LILA Vous m'avez pratiquement aveuglée et je ne devrais pas m'inquéter?

INCONNU Ce n'est qu'un reflet de la lune qui apparaît et disparaît alternant mystère et clarté entre les nuages nocturnes déchirés par le vent.

LILA *(ironique)* Quel poète! C'est à vomir!

INCONNU Faut ce qu'il faut ... chérie. Et puis, tout est tellement confus dans ces anfractuosités du temps, comme si rien n'existait vraiment, et pourtant, existait en même temps ... Vous comprenez? *(ambigu)* Existait!

LILA Oh, non!

INCONNU Oh, si! Et c'est pourquoi la poésie aide à saisir les nuances les plus essentielles, à sublimer toute chose, pour ne pas transformer le chaos dans lequel nous sommes plongés en une petite orgie de quatre sous où l'excitation produit deux jouissances à peine, un orgasme ridicule de petite morveuse à ses premier attouchements.

LILA Schämen Sie sich! Vous n'avez pas honte?

INCONNU Heureusement, il y a la poésie. Grâce à elle, la conscience est sauvée, l'oreille n'est plus importunée, et la langue tourne sept fois dans la bouche ... Tout se résout en une méga branlette linguistique. Heureuse?

LILA Qu'est-ce que ça peut vois faire? De toute manière, je ne vous parle plus, vous êtes trop vulgaire.

INCONNU N'ayez pas peur, bientôt il fera jour. Et tout prendra fin.

LILA Vraiment?

INCONNU oui, oui, vous verrez: les mauvais rêves s'évanouiront.

LILA Et vous reprendrez votre route? Croyez-moi, j'en serai soulagée!

INCONNU Vous m'associez donc à un cauchemar. Merci. C'est gentil. C'est entendu: dès que le soleil se lève – s'il se lève – je m'évapore. Promis. Et chose promise chose due.

LILA Comment cela s'il se lève?

INCONNU Simple hypothèse.

LILA Pourquoi? Le soleil pourrait ne plus se lever?

INCONNU Oh, non! vous me prenez pour un idiot? Comment voulez-vous que je ne le sache pas; tôt au tard, il finira bien par se lever, ainsi qu'il le fait depuis des centaines de millions d'années?

LILA Qu'entendez-vous par là, alors?

INCONNU Que l'un de nous deux pourrait ne jamais revoir le soleil. Vous y avez pensé?

LILA Mail il ne manque que quelques minutes ... *(saisie de doute)* Vous êtes un assassin?

INCONNU Ma chérie! Le plus grand assassin, notre pire ennemi, c'est le destin! C'est lui qui commande. Je n'y suis pour rien, moi, j'obéis! J'obéis et je me bats. Parfois, je ne comprends pas, mais je me conforme. En d'autres termes: je succombe, si je dois succomber. Et pareil pour vous.

LILA Pour moi?

INCONNU Bien sûr. Parce que, par exemple, si le destin a décidé que dans dix secondes vous mourrez – d'un infarctus, par example – puvez-vous vous y opposer? vous révolter? vous défendre? Essayez! Allez-y, montrez moi ... Démenez-vous, agitez-vous, dandinez-vous! Allez, tapez là, ici, je suis le destin, giflez-moi, résistez! Vous voyez? Vous ne pouvez pas.

LILA Moi? Dans dix secondes?

INCONNU ... dix, neuf (c'est fou ce que le temps file, parfois!) ... six, cinq ... (qu'est-ce qu'une seconde? Ça semble rien, mais en une seconde naissent et meurent des millions, des milliards de micro-organismes!) ... trois, deux, un, zéro! Vous vous sentez bien?

LILA Oui, je crois ... j'espère!

INCONNU Alors le destin n'a pas encore décidé de votre sort. D'ailleurs, on ne peut pas le forcer. D'autant que les Parques, qui son en enfer, tissent la vie des êtres humains, ont leur propre rythme de production, et elles ne sont que trois pour tour le genre humain. Vous comprendrez ...

LILA J'aimerais, mais alors vraiment, vous mettre un gros coup de poing dans votre sale gueule monstrueuse.

INCONNU D'accord. Moquez-vous de moi. Ou préféreriez-vous que je m'évapore comme un rêve au réveil? On se frotte les yeux, on prend un café et ... à propos, et mon café?

LILA Oui, si vous arrêtez vos bavardages!

INCONNU Hélan pour vous, je ne suis pas un rêve. Peut-être un conte de fée en chair et en os, mais un rêve ...

LILA Mon dieu, je ne vous supporte plus!

INCONNU *(il se retire)* S'il vous plaît, ne le nommez pas en vain. Un peu de respect. Si ce n'est pas pour lui, au moins pour moi.

LILA *(comme possédée)* Parfois, j'ai l'impression de saisir une lueur de vérité, puis tout m'échappe à nouveau, et je me perds sans savoir quel chemin je dois chercher en moi pout en sortir ...

INCONNU Vaut-il vraiment mieux savoir? Réfléchissez bien ...

LILA Je ne sais pas. Cela dépend de quoi.

INCONNU De ce qui agite votre organe cérébral, jaillissant par moment des abîmes de vostre conscience, telle une vague souterraine qui se brise sur la côte de votre «Je», élevant vers le ciel des giclées de lave brûlante.

LILA Votre psyc ... psychisme (encore un mot que je ne connaissais pas) est plus tordu que le mien.

INCONNU Très tordu, je le reconnais. Essayez de défaire le nœud coulant de ma conscience et vous vous retrouverez indissolublement liée aux plombs qui m'entraînent vers le fond, dans cet immense tourbillon où vous venez d'entrevoir, dans votre rêve ... la Bête!

LILA Maudite Bête! Maudit ... vous!

INCONNU Mieux vaut, croyez-moi, et d'espère que suivrez mon conseil, mieux vaut se tenir sous contrôle, verrouillé, comme au couvent.

LILA Ou comme le contenu de votre valise. Je serais vraiment curieuse de ...

INCONNU Oh non, ne l'ouvrez pas, ne l'ouvrez jamais. Considérez cette valise comme votre âme: ce qui se trouve à l'intérieur, une fois à la lumière, pourrait vous anéantir. Qui sait quelles mauvaises surprises pourraient en sortir ...

LILA De cette valise? Un alliage de métaux, vous l'avez dit vous-même, créé dans un stupide laboratoire militaire où ils fabriquent uniquement des monstruosités...

INCONNU Mais oui, mais oui ...

LILA Ou bien y a-t-il autre chose?

INCONNU Dans votre psychisme aussi il y a autre chose ... quelque chose d'artificiel, comme une usine à feux d'artifice où une étincelle suffit pour libérer une réaction en chaîne aux conséquences désastreuses. Une boîte de Pandore, croyez-moi.

LILA Vous m'effrayez.

INCONNU Et moi je vous prie de ne pas vous effrayer, cela n'en vaut pas la peine. Nous sommes assis sur une bombe atomique? Et alors ? tant qu'elle n'explose pas ... Nous pouvons même faire l'amour dessus, si nous en avons envie. Un monstre nous habite? Il suffit de le laisser tranquille dans un coin et qu'il ne nous les casse pas (excusez-moi) avec ses aboiements bestiaux. Et puis, finalement, qu'est-ce que l'existence? Un fol éclat qui, l'espace d'un instant, erre dans la nuit des temps. Pourquoi gâcher une fête déjà si courte? Suivez mon conseil: jouissez de la vie tant que vous le pouvez. Et n'y pensez plus.

LILA Je ne devrais plus penser à quoi?

INCONNU A quoi? A la Bête!

LILA Tantôt elle hurle, elle rugit comme une hyène en proie aux morsures de la faim, tantôt elle grince des dents, prête à s'élancer. Facile de ne pas y penser!

INCONNU Imaginez que votre esprit est comme ma valise, c'est-à-dire vide, jusqu'à ce quenois y mettions quelque chose, moi dans ma valise, vous dans votre esprit. D'accord?

LILA Peut-être ... peut-être est-ce moi qui ne suis pas à la hauteur, à votre hauteur ... une petite fille méchante, taquine ... je ne suis que cela ... que prétendez-vous de moi, comment voulez-vous que je puisse rivaliser avec un ... un

INCONNU Avec un diable?

LILA oui, oui, excusez-moi.

INCONNU Ne vous excusez pas. Chacun voit le choses à sa façon. Et si vous me voyez en diable, eh bien, oui, je le suis. Heureuse?

LILA Je voudrais ne jamais vous avoir rencontré, je voudrais que votre voiture se soit cassée loin d'ici, je voudrais que vous n'ayez pas vu la lumière, je voudrais que les chasseurs arrivent pour prendre leur petit déjeuner ...

INCONNU Vous oubliez une chose dans ce Pater Noster écœurant: *(en imitant sa voix)* Je voudrais que le monstre n'existe pas, ou, s'il existe, qu'il n'ait pas commis ses atrocités. Non?

LILA Vous avez décidé de me faire mourir de peur?

INCONNU Peur, vous?

LILA Oui, moi. Peur de moi-même, de ce que j'ai fait, de ce que je pourrais faire et ferai très certainement, et de ce que je ne peux pas ne pas faire. Alors, l'angoisse se déchaîne en moi et jaillit hors de moi comme la mousse d'une bouteille de bière agitée, recouvrant les choses, les personnes ... tout!

INCONNU Ce sont les symptômes, les racines du mal que vous couvez en vous: cette Bête. Il vous faudrait l'intuition sans la compréhension, car la connaissance pleine et complète de soi peut conduire, c'est même inévitable, au fond du gouffre du désespoir. Bien sûr, l'intuition inconsciente est difficile, mais elle est encore possible.

Comprendre sans savoir ... dans le but évident, de détruire l'animal que nois sommes, sans détruire notre âme, en la mettant en morceaux inutilement. Vous demanderez: comment faire? Eh bien, je suis là, moi. Laissez-moi me concentrer un instant et vous verrez!

LILA *(après une pause)* Vous êtes de penser à une femme nue? Eh, mais c'est moi! Et je me touche! Je ne veux pas, cochon! Qu'est-ce que je fais dans vos pensées?

INCONNU Chacun sa façon de se concentrer. L'un fume une cigarette, l'autre ... bref, ne vous immiscez pas dans mes fantasmes érotiques. Je suis tout de même libre de ...

LILA Mais comment ai-je pu voir au dedans de vous? Au dedans de moi?

INCONNU Chut!

LILA Mon Dieu! Vous pensez au dedans de moi! Dedans!

INCONNU Silence!

Il s'efforce de se concentrr, mais cette opération produit une série d'effets étranges, paranormaux, du genre: bruits, éclairs, images qui giclent rapides sur les murs, ombres. A la fin, la scène d'un accouplement brutal et bouleversant entre deux monstres qui génèrent un petit monstre horrible.

INCONNU Vous avez vu? Entendu? Senti? Satisfaite? Vous avez joui?

LILA Et moi j'aurais ... dedans ... en moi ... cette ... cette ordure?

INCONNU Voure pire. Je n'au cueilli que quelques fleurs, par ci, par là, en passant! Disons: le meilleur de votre production intérieure. Goethe aurait eu besoin d'un millier de pages (qu'est-ce qu'il a traîné en longueur avec son homunculus), par contre, moi, je n'y vais pas par quatre chemins: peu de mots, et des faits parlant. Lire, d'accord, mais tant qu'on ne s'y cogne pas la tête on n'y croit pas ...

LILA Je suis tellement sans défense face à moi-même ...

INCONNU Et c'est pour ça que vous pleurez? Vous n'avez pas l'impression d'exagérer? Il est vrai qu'il n'y a pas de pire mal que ce qui vient de nous ... mais on trouve une solution à tout, croyez-moi.

LILA Non, je ne crois pas.

INCONNU Ne désespérez. Au fond, votre gouffre intérieur n'est pas plus obscur ou plus barbare que celui de vos semblables. On creuse on creuse et on se retrouve toujours à l'âge de pierre! Comment, me demandé-je, vous n'avez pas fait de pas de géant en ces ... combien déjà? – bon, on ne va pas tous les recompter, trois mille ans d'histoire? Et vous êtes restés si primitifs, si bestiaux, hommes des cavernes?

LILA Moi non, non, ou du moins je ne savais pas que j'étais comme vous dites.

INCONNU Sans doute aurait-il mieux valu ne pas savoir, ne pas voir, ne pas entendre, comme les trois singes. Si le «Je» n'entendait pas ce que dit le Moi, si le Moi ne voyait pas ce que fait la Conscience, et si la Conscience taisait ce que font les deux autres, on serait mieux ici qu'au Paradis, vous pouvez me croire.

LILA C'est trop angoissant, arrêtez!

INCONNU Pourtant, vos peurs ancestrales, se matérialisent en pensées – lesquelles se concrétisent à leur tour en des images qui ensuite s'incarnent, donnant vie aux relations charnelles (d'une manière ou d'une autre, on revient toujours à ça, la chair; la chair faible, certes, mais tellement bonne) – j'ai perdu le fil, je disais?

LILA Mes peurs ancestrales ...

INCONNU Justement ... elles sont agrandies par la nuit comme des ombrs monstrueuses projetées sur le murs de votre «Je». Si une fourmi traverse la loupe d'un projecteur, elle apparaîtra sur l'écran en monstre préhistorique, une créature infernal, et – naïvement – vous penserez voir le diable en personne. Mais en réalité, qu'est-ce que c'était?

LILA Rien.

INCONNU Exactement, rien. Idem pour les cauchemars qui semblent insupportables pendant le sommeil et qu'au réveil, on souhaiterait effacer de son esprit. Que représentent-ils en réalité, si ce n'est qu'une fraction minime, quelques instants, de notre nirvana nocturne? Et nour devrions nous laisser gâcher la vie par ces quelques poignées de seconde où l'esprit s'emballe, se cabre et brûle le bitume avant de tirer les freins inhibiteurs?

LILA Je ne sais pas ... je ne sair plus quoi faire!

INCONNU Je viens de vous le dire: rien. Laissez tomber les silhouettes suggérées par une fugue de lumières, aperçus d'infini, images abstraites poussées vers le ciel gris de l'âme qui, parfois, semble vouloir nous suffoquer dans notre berceau (moi aussi j'ai été enfant, et je me souviens de l'angoisse de ces jours encore «bestiaux» où la conscience de soi, l'âme était un conteneur vide, un interrupteur éteint). D'autres fois, il a le pouvoir de nois élever dans des sphères célestes grâce à un tourbillon spirituel, à un processus de sublimation intérieur. C'est un peu comme le vin, qui mûrit avec le temps et se transforme de moût en nectar, à la fois divin et diabolique, puisque il n'y a pas de dieux sans démons. Et vice-versa.

LILA Pourvu que ce vin ne tourne pas au vinaigre.

INCONNU Il nous appartient de ne pas le faire tourner. Tout est là.

LILA Alors expliquez-moi comment vous faites pour plonger dans les méandres de mon esprit.

INCONNU Non, non, vous me prenez pour qui? Primo, j'en serais bien incapable. Deuxio, pour quelle raison devrais-je le faire?

LILA *(agressive)* Que se passe-t-il, alors?

INCONNU Tout simplement, vous pensez à ce que je suis en train de dire, vous le pensez en même temps que moi et vous croyez que je suce vos idées, comme un vampire, comme une sangsue *(il cherche à l'embrasser sur le cou)* comme un suçon.

LILA *(se retire)* Et?

INCONNU Il n'y a pas de «et» : ce sont des banalités, des choses anodines, à votre portée. Vous croyez penser ce que je pense ou que je pense ce que vous pensez. Tout simplement parce que j'exprime des concepts somme toute évidents. Universaux!, c'est-à-dire valables pour le genre humain.

LILA Quelle chance!

INCONNU Ne vous inquiétez pas, je ne suis pas aussi diabolique que je peux le paraîre.

LILA Sans doute ... mais vous boitez!

INCONNU Moi? Vraiment? Je ne m'en étais jamais aperçu. Je dois faire contrôler mes sabots.

LILA Et votre pied gauche est plus gros que le droit. On dirait qu'il va éclater dans votre chaussure.

INCONNU C'est le pied avec lequel je pousse le frein inhibiteur. J'ai dû trop pousser ces derniers temps ... *(il enlève sa chaussure, montre un pied monstreux)*

LILA Mais vous avez une patte de chèvre à la place du pied!

INCONNU Et alors ? (il remet vite sa chaussure). Vous êtes raciste? Vous n'aimez ceux qui sont un peu différents? Regardez-vous dans le miroir: vous aussi vous avez un grain de beauté très laid dans le cou. Mais moi, comme je suis bien élevé, je ne l'ai pas fait remarquer. On est d'accord, dès que vous irez chez le dermatologue, j'irai chez le cordonnier pour ma chaussure.

LILA Vous avez raison de vous moquer de moi. J'ai eu tort, vraiment.

INCONNU Oui, il n'y a pas beaucoup de lumière ... et votre imagination doit vous avoir joué un mauvais tour. Vous alors, vous voyez des monstres partout, c'est une obsession ! Même en moi, qui me suis bien conduit, jusqu'ici (à part ces marques sur le bras: un excès d'animalité dont parfois je suis la proie), malgré le fait que j'aurais pu profiter de la situation pour satisfaire mes envies, si j'en avais eu, et il n'est pas dit que je n'ai aurai pas. J'ai réussi à les maîtriser suffisamment, non?

LILA *(nerveuse, va à la fenêtre)* Mais où est-il passé, le soleil ? Cette nuit si froide ... elle dure une éternité.

Sans se faire remarquer, l'Inconnu boit deux bouteilles de marc, s'empiffre de tout ce qu'il trouve, vole de la monnaie du tiroir, se cure le nez et colle la saluté sous le comptoir, pète et renifle satisfait du résultat. Pendant ce temps, Lila à la fenêtre tambourine sur la vitre.

INCONNU Si je peux me permette: l'éternité est une asbstraction, un produit ambigu de l'esprit humain qui, dans ses limites et sa contingence, se construit exprès un infini aussi hypothétique qu'inexistant. Comme si l'infini était une simple succession de point géométriques (ou mathématiques) à atteindre et à mettre dans son escarcelle, un âne de Buridan qui n'arrêterait pas de chier des monnaies d'or. Eh bien, non ! L'erreur est de considérer l'éternité en sens quantitatif et non pas qualitatif. L'instant est éternel, pas l'ensemble des instants. Atteindre l'infini signifie pouvoir dire à l'Instant, au Moment, comme le fait Faust, «arrête-toi, c'est beau » au lieu de « quel ennui, dépêche-toi de passer ». Prenez mon cas, par exemple, moi aussi je suis passé dans ce coin et, attiré par une force irrésistible – l'envie d'un café – je me suis arrêté. Et j'attends depuis une éternité.

LILA D'où venez-vous?

INCONNU Vous voulez vraiment le savoir? *(ambigu)* Je viens d'un lieu que vous ne connaissez pas ... et je suis sûr que vous ne désirez pas le connaître. Donc ... laissez tomber, il vaut mieux, pour vous!

LILA De l'autre côté de la frontière?

INCONNU Bien au delà. Même trop.

LILA Que de mystères!

INCONNU Que serait la vie sans un peu de mystère?

LILA Rien. Vous avez raison.

INCONNU C'est cela, un met fade ... Mais là, j'ai besoin de pisser ... Vous permettez? Où sont les toilettes?

LILA Au fond à gauche ... Attendez, c'est fermé. Je dois vous donner la clef ... Mince *(fouille dans un tiroir)* où est-elle ?

INCONNU Dépêchez-vous, j'ai la prostate un peu faible.

LILA Je ne la trouve pas ... *(cherche)* On garde la porte fermée pour éviter que des drogués viennent se shooter ... hélas, la drogue est arrivée jusqu'ici ... pauvre jeunesse!

INCONNU Je m'en fous.

LILA Voilà, ça y est!

INCONNU *(prend brusquement la clé)* Donnez ... *(il s'achemine du mauvais côté)*

LILA J'ai dit à gauche, Links!

INCONNU *(en maniant nerveusement la serrure)* Sale monde, je suis passé dans la cuisine ... en suivant l'odeur ... Dans cette auberge les fourneaux et les casseroles puent plus que les chiottes.

LILA *(seule)* Seule avec un fou pareil! Il tient de ces propos ... Brr, j'en ai la chair de poule! *(regarde par la fenêtre)*. Et aujourd'hui, personne à l'horizon, pas même les habitués du café-calva (bien arrosé, mais, chut!, ça ne se dit pas au petit matin). D'habitude, à cette heure-ci, ils frappent aux vitres et se font passer le plateau à l'extérieur, pour ne pas avoir à enlever leur veste et attacher leur chien (je ne les fais jamais entrer, ces sales bêtes baveuses) ... ce matin, par contre, personne, niemand, comme si ... comme si le monstre ... il ne manquait plus que le monstre ! Comme si les affaires n'allaient pas suffisamment mal comme cela ...

La porte des toilettes s'ouvre. Lila ne peut pas s'en apercevoir et continue à regarder dehors dans l'attente que quelqu'un arrive. L'Inconnu est en train de pisser. Mais il s'agit d'une pissade diabolique, dont le bruit monte justqu'aux décibels d'une cascade. Ensuite, la chasse qui se vide se transforme en un tourbillon effroyable. Lila est embêtée par ce vacarme bestial.

LILA Ça fait un moment que vous êtes enfermé là-dedans ... Vous allez bien?

INCONNU Il fait jour?

LILA Pas encore ... *(à elle-même)* bizarre ... *(à lui)* pourquoi?

INCONNU Je vais bien alors, ne vous inquiétez pas. J'ai juste pas mal de boutons à reboutonner ... Mon costume est à l'ancienne ... Une sorte d'armure, un peu carnavalesque, mais je l'aime bien. Et puis c'est confortable ... sauf lorsqu'on doit sortir son zizi! Mais je ne pense pas que vous ayez ce genre de problèmes ... Allez, rentre, sale bête!

LILA Vous vous en prenez à qui?

INCONNU Un ami.

Entre-temps, l'atmosphère de la toilette est envahie d'une étrange vapeur rougeâtre qui sort de la cuvette. Tour cela accompagné d'étranges bruit : vagissements, cris, crépitements et lueurs infernales.

INCONNU Je suis la côté sombre de la lumière
Celui qui lève son regard vers Dieu
Et ose mettre à nu la vérité.
Ce Dieu qui a imposé sept plaies à l'humanité.
Ce Dieu qui a imposé à Abraham le sacrifice,
Inhumain, de son fils aîné chéri,
Ce Dieu qui a condamné sa créature,
La chair de son esprit, à l'agonie sur la croix,
Qui a laissé à l'homme comme seul héritage
Pour freiner son ambition d'éternité:
La mort, en échange de la vie dans un au delà
Qui n'existe pas car il existe à peine un en deça,
Ce Dieu là, vous le considérez encore comme votre Seigneur le Père?
Bien, alors ce Dieu c'est moi, Baphomet,
Et il n'y a d'autre Dieu que moi!
Quelle belle arnaque que de faire croire
A l'esprit sot de l'homme
Qu'il est entre le bien et le mal,
Qu'il peut choisir, comme si la décision lui appartenait.
Toi, homme, tu n'es qu'un pauvre idiot
A qui le serpent n'a accordé qu'une morsure:
Tu as compliqué ta vie en acceptant
Ce jeu de massacre avec ce Créateur
Qui t'a mis dans le jardin du monde,
Comme un jouet, justement,
Histoire s'amuser avec de temps en temps.
Moi, moi, moi, moi seul je suis ton Dieu!
Il n'y a pas d'autre Dieu que moi!
(souriant) Signé: Baphomet

En écho, les hurlements des loups, parmi lesquels on remarque une voix.

La lamentation du loup solitaire

L'homme est un loup pour l'homme,
Et il n'y a de bête pire que lui.

Moi, d'ordures je dois me nourrir,
Lui, tire sur qui a des ailes.
Dieu à son image l'a créé,
Puis son âme vraie a dévoilé
En diable il s'est mué
De soi le croyant différent.
Mais quels montres se cachent dans l'obscurité
Que son imagination n'ait pas fabriqués ?
Les ombres sur les murs sont une pure folie
Qui transforme la réalité en manie.
Attention, Lila, au monstre sournois
Il s'est caché en toi
De toutes tes forces repousse-le
Si tu ne veux qu'en obsédée il te transforme.

LILA *(énervée par les hurlements)* Sales et maudites bêtes! Il ne manquait plus que cela pour me rendre folle! Quand il gèle, elles s'approchent des centres habités pout fouiller dans les poubelles et chercher à manger. Ce ne sont plus des loups, mais des hyènes, des êtres dégoûtants, dénaturés, des zombies plus repoussants et visqueux que des serpents. Plus ils ont faim, plus ils deviennent impertinents, impudents; ils défien même les chasseurs et cherchent à pénétrer dans les maisons ... Ils savent prendre un aspect vaguement humain, si bien que la nuit, on parvient difficilement à les reconnaître, malgré leurs longues dents pointues et leurs oreilles poilues ... Je me méfie de lui ... Il tient de ces propos! Il est si ambigu! Et si c'était le loup, c'est-à-dire le monstre? Qui peut savoir ce qu'il y a dans sa valise ... *(elle la traîne sur scène)* Bon sang, ça pèse des tonnes! Arrête, Lila, freine ton imagination, pourquoi des pensées si mauvaises? Que veux-tu qu'il y ait là-dedans? Ce doit être un scientifique et il a des livres avec lui ... mais pouquoi ne les a-t-il pas laissés dans sa voiture? Et cette histoire de gallium! Comment y croire! Je ne suis pas stupide! *(saisie de doute)* Et si c'était le monstre? Si, à l'intérieur, il y avait le corps de sa dernière victime, découpé en morceaux congelés et flissés dans des sacs plastioques? Mon Dieu! Je ne peux plus supporter ce doute, je dois absolument savoir. Parce que, si c'était un monstre, un vrai, une sorte de loup, je pourrais être sa prochaine victime. Qui peut savoir ce qu'il a en tête? D'ailleurs, il n'y a pas de mal si je jette un coup d'œil, juste pour être sûre que je n'ai pas affaire à ... mais il faut faire vite, Lila, vite, avant qu'il revienne ...

L'Inconnu apparait derrière son dos, à nouveau normal. Il assiste à la scène en silence et sans se faire remarquer, avec un rictus de satisfaction, comme s'il voulait que Lila fouille vraiment dans ses affaires. Lila ouvre les serrures en murmurant :

LILA Komisch, c'est ouvert ...

Puis elle ouvre lentement la valise, comme si elle craignait que quelque chose puisse en sortir, une surprise monstrueuse (accompagnée par les bruits adéquats). Au fur et à mesure que le couvercle se lève, le visage de Lila est envahi d'une lumière rouge-sang venant de la valise d'où sort aussi de la fumée méphitique et colorée. Lila reste quelques instants à observer l'effroyable contenu de la valise, qu'elle referme aussitôt d'un coup en criant.

LILA Noooon!
INCONNU Alors, le spectacle vous a plu, mademoiselle? Qu'est-ce tu espérais y trouver, hein? des fleurs?
LILA Cette lumière sinistre dans votre regard ... Quelle idiote ... ne pas comprendre ... ce que, ce qui se cachait derrière vos mots étranges, vos propos ambigus ... le monstre, le maniaque!
INCONNU Vous pouvez dire: le psychopathe! Cela ne me vexe pas.
LILA Ne me touchez pas, ne vous approchez pas! Au secours!
INCONNU C'est de ta faute. Tu as voulu fourrer ton nez dans ma valise, et c'est comme si tu avais découvert ce à quoi ta conscience faisait obstacle: poum! et le champagne, le nectar des dieux et des démons est sorti agité par tes petites mains te salissant telle la semence d'un monstre. Et maintenant, jouis, jouis!
LILA C'est dégoûtant!
INCONNU Poum! Regarde, allez, regarde dedans. *(il la force à regarder dans la valise)*
LILA Non, laisse-moi tranquille, je ne suis pas méchante, je ne suois pas un monstre!
INCONNU Arrête-toi, c'est beau, arrête-toi, c'est beau! *(il rit)*

L'Inconnu sort de sa valise une véritable collection d'échantillon d'objets de sex-shop, en les endossant ou forçant Lila de les toucher, etc. Pendant ce temps, de la machine à café commence à sortir une vapeur très dense qui enveloppe lentement la scène en la faisant disparaître.

INCONNU Le psychisme est une machine à pression : si toutes les soupapes sont bouchées, tôt ou tard ça dégénère. Et tu es une dégénérée!

LILA Ce n'est pas vrai!

INCONNU Ah non? Et ce phallus en latex très souple à deux pointes pour les doubles pénétrations, tu n'en as pas rêvé, cette nuit, quand tu te faisais un solitaire sous tes couvertures?

LILA Ça suffit, démon, je t'en prie *(elle chantonne hystérique tandis que la scène est entiprement envahie de vapeur)*

Le rêve de mes pensées

Toutes de noir-foncé

Connaît bien les tourments

Qui m'agitent en dedans.

Je suis seule et j'ai peur,

Ma part d'ombre me rend pleine de frayeur.

Des flashs rapides où il dévoile son aspect monstreux. Puis, parmi les cris de désespoir de Lila et les rires de Baphomet, pour quelques moments, NOIR.

Lettre ouverte à un monstre quelconque

Lila lit :

Cher monstre,

Je baigne dans une souffrance inouïe, dans une douleur sans mesure, autour de moi il n'y a qu'un silence pénible. Mais je reste dans l'attente d'un signe, d'un message – suggéré par tes appels à l'aide – qui me permettrait de communiquer avec toi, d'une façon ou d'une autre.

Je me demande comment tu peux vivre avec les fantasmes de ta cruauté, avec ce sentiment de culpabilité qui, j'en suis certain, te colle à la peau. Je me demande si tu arrives et, comment, à rejeter l'angoisse et le trouble qui ne peuvent pas t'atteindre, grâce à ton patrimoine d'humanité, que je te reconnais. Tu m'as agressée dans mon intimité la plus profonde, dans mon amour le plus authentique et je me demande, avec obsession, pourquoi?

Je m'interroge dans un cauchemar sans fin : « combien a-t-il souffert? Qu'a-t-il dit? Qu'a-t-il crié pendant que tu le torturais? » Je me demande comment était son regard quando il rencontrait tes yeux ... implorant? Terrifié? Effaré? Ou bien étonné d'une méchanceté si inconnue et insoupçonnée? Ds-le moi, de quelque manière, dis-moi ce que tu éprouves, ce que tu ressens, comment tu peux vivre et faire semblant de rien, continuer à rester parmi les gens, avec tes amis, continuer à travailler, à t'amuser avec, en toi, le souvenir d'un crime, l'image d'une petite victime sacrifiée si bêtement à ton égoïsme?

Je voudrais te regarder dans les yeux et comprendre – oui, comprendre ! – ce que tu ressens maintenant, s'il ya en toi le désir de te libérer de ce geste qui marque ton existence, si le sentiment intime d'échec, d'inutilité de ton acte te tourmente, tout comme la réalité de la mort m'accable.

Aide-moi au moins à comprendre, fais-moi voir qu'il n'est pas vrai que tu es un monstre, mais bien un être délaissé qui malgré le mal causé, pour des raisons différentes, est lié à moi d'une même souffrance : l'offense faite à notre être.

Fais en sorte que le silence ne devienne le destruction de tour sentiment.

Un monstre nommé Lila

Une brève apparition de Baphomet
(habillé en show man il fait quelques jeux de prestidigitateur, sur une musique de cirque)

Devinez la devinette:
Qu'est que ceci, qu'est que cela ?
Ouvre bien tes oreilles
Même si tu trouves stupide
d'écouter des choses déjà dites
Donc ...
Cela semble souvent une arcane,
L'esprit humain le perçoit
Mais il reste inteerdit au profane
Qui cherche soi même en vain
et n'a que sable plein la main.
Sais-tu quoi? Sais-tu qoui ? Sais-tu quoi?
Trois secondes pour répondre tu as
Ou en enfer avec moi tu iras
Un, deux ... trois?
Comment? Vous me faites rire!
Vous n'avex pas compris?
Mais c'est l'infini!
Bon, bon, bon:

Encore une fois.
Qu'est-ce que c'est
Qu'on a mis quand on l'a enlevé?
Rien? Allons S'il vous plaît!
Vous n'avez pas compris?
C'est le doigt du perroquet
Qui dans le bus touche le cul coquet!
Bon, bon, bon:
Deux à zéro pour moi.
Je viendrais vous chercher
Une fois fini de jouer
Mais d'abord mon café.

La scène s'est transformée en l'intérieur d'une cellule. Sur le fond est restée la grande fenêtre, mais fermée par un lourd grillage. C'est la nuit : on aperçoit de la fenêtre une lune immense, obsédante, presque animée. Lila est assise sur un lit, recroquevillée contre le mur, les genoux dans ses bras et le regard figé. Elle chantonne.

LILA Le vide de mes pensées
Toutes de noir-foncé
Connaît bien les tourments
Qui m'agitent en dedans.
Je suis seule et j'ai peur,
Ma part d'ombre me rend pleine de frayeur.

Soudain, la lune se transforme. Elle rougit, des cornes lui poussent et – par une surimpression d'images projetées par derrière, elle devient Baphomet, le diable.

BAPHOMET-LUNE Bonjour, Lila!
LILA Bonjour, lune.
BAPHOMET-LUNE Comment vas-tu?
LILA Comme d'habitude. Mal. Déprimée.
BAPHOMET-LUNE Je vois. Mais pourquoi cela, la vie est tellement belle!
LILA Je suis méchante. Pour moi, elle est mauvaise. Un cauchemar.
BAPHOMET-LUNE Allons donc ... Tu aimerais sortir de là? Nous pourrions aller à la Foire du trône, jouer ... dans le tunnel des monstres, par exemple. Ce serait beau. Ouah! Quel pied!
LILA Non, tu veux seulement me faire souffrir. Toujours plus.

BAPHOMET-LUNE Mais non, mais non, je veux t'aider, te remonter le moral, crois-moi, trouver une explication, une solution, une issue, apaiser tes souffrances, autrement trop infernales ...

LILA Pitié, aidex-moi, je ne veux pas recommencer, je ne veux plus faire de mal, gardez-moi enfermée ... verrouillée ... et jetez la clé. Et toi, va-t-en, maudite bête!

BAPHOMET-LUNE Alors, je ne viendrais plus te voir. A bientôt! On ne se libère pas si facilment de soi-même, de son propre démon, celui qui niche en dedans, et qui est toujours en éveil pour profiter des faiblesses de la conscience. Non, Lila, è bientôt! C'est la vie ...

La lune redevient normale. Lila se lève d'un bond, va au miroir et commence à faire des grimaces, à s'arracher la chair, à se gifler.

LILA Qui es-tu, hein? Qui es-tu? Un monstre? Un homme? Un animal ou un être humain? Une bête ou toi-même? Tu comprends? Tu m'entends? Tu m'entends? *(se gifle hysthériquement)* je te parle, ma petite! *(elle prend une voix de petite fille)* Maman, maman, qu'est-ce que c'est que cette chose rouge, qu'est-ce que c'est? du sang? *(voix adulte)* Combien de fois je t'ai dit de ne pas te toicher là? Ne te touches jamais plus, se toucher c'est mal, c'est Satan! *(elle pleure sur le lit)*

On entend des pas. Quelqu'un manie des lourdes clés, la serrure se déclenche ; des nombreux, et même trop nombreux tours de clés, comme dans un cauchemar. Même le grincement qui accompagne la porte qui s'ouvre doit être souligné, voire gênant (mais nécessaire au sens où le moindre événement joue ici rôle psychologique, c'est-à-dire amplifié). Entre Baphomet (alias l'Inconnu avec le masque du Diable).

INCONNU Bonsoir, mademoiselle.

LILA Toi?

INCONNU Hélas pour toi, mais hélas un peu pour moi aussi, je suis enfermé dans tes mécanisme mentaux. J'aimerais bien en sortir, aller me balader, prendre un peu d'air au lieu de respirer l'atmosphère méphitique de cet égout intérieur, mais je ne peux pas: je suis ton prisonnier.

LILA Non, c'est moi qui suis la prisonnière.

INCONNU Que veux-tu que je te dise? Je suis ta créature et c'est tout. C'est la vérité que tu le veuilles ou non.

LILA Prouve-le.

INCONNU Si. Pense seulement à moi, et j'existe. Arrête, et je disparais. Cela dépend de toi Lila, de toile Mal que tu mei fais représenter. Malgré moi. Satan existe, oui, mais dans l'homme, son créateur même. Et toi, tu m'as créé à partir de rien: Criminelle! Regarde, regarde comme je suis laid, regarde comme je suis monstreux, je suis dégoûtant; mais tu m'as forgé à ton image, monstre que tu es!

Lila chatonne son refrain se bouchant les oreilles pour ne pas entendre.

Le cygne de mes pensées
Toutes de nor-foncé
Connaît bien les tourments
Qui m'agitent en dedans.
Je suis seule et j'ai peur, ma part d'ombre me rend plein de frayeur.

Elle est comme endiablée, se débat hystériquement comme en proie à des convulsions épilectiques.

INCONNU C'est le moment: son voyage intérieur s'est achevé par une chute de l'esprit: l'âme est arrivée à destination dans le royaume des ténèbres. C'est le moment! Elle est prête pour le dernier saut dans son enfer, où le côte bestial de son être se promènera sans obstacles, indomptable, prêt à perpétrer son mal. *(à elle)* Regarde-toi dans le miroir, Lila, maintenant tu es prête, maintenant je te reconnais.
LILA *(se regarde dans le miroir et s'aperçoit qu'elle s'est transformée en un monstre)* Nooon!
BAPHOMET *(il porte sur scène les appareils pour l'électrochoc, et tout en parlant il connecte les câbles au corps et à la tête de Lila)* Il n'y a pas d'issue lorsqu'on se damne, quand on s'enferme volontairement dan un enfer mental. Peut-être que le mal dont on doit guérir ... inatteignable, au dessus de toute chose, impassible. Dans ce néant il n'y a pas dc Dieu pas de péché, juste l'inexorable temps jamais vécu jamais à vivre. Abstrait, inconnu, vide. Tu comprends ? Non ? C'est pareil. Descendons, Lila, encore plus bas, dans le noir de ta conscience, nous en avons presque touché le fond, là où la lumière de la raison s'efface devant une autre lumière, noire, celle de la nuit des temps. Tu égares ta propre étincelle ... (sa voix, persuasive, s'éloigne de plus en plus tandis que les lumières baissent) Adieu, Lila, adieu ... (il donne une décharge, Lila sursaute. Il double la charge, Lila devient rigide comme un condamné à mort tué sur la chaise électrique)
Noir.

Dernière apprition de Baphomet
Epilogue
_Baphomet, sur son trône en enfer, lit un livre ancien, tandis que Lila,
désormais diablesse, accomplit des obscénités à ses pieds._

« Se considérant comme le chef-d'œuvre de la Divinité, l'homme
pourrait nois apparaître – plus qu'aucune autre créature – comme la
preuve de l'incapacité ou de la méchanceté du prétendu Créateur. Dans
cet être sensible, intelligent, pensant, qui se croit l'objet de l'amour
divin, et qui forge son Dieu à son image, nous ne voyons qu'une
machine frêle, défectueuse, exposée aux pannes. Ne vaudrait-il pas
mieux être une machine inanimée, plutôt qu'un être inquiet et
superstitieux qui doit trembler sous le joug de son Dieu, à l'idée des
peines infinies qui l'attendent dans la vie future? » Qu'en dis-tu, Lila,
hein? Le vieux Spinoza, n'a-t-il pas raison? Y a-t-il une vie future? Y a-
t-il un espoir pour l'homme? Et, si oui, lequel?
LILA Miaooo!
BAPHOMET Très bien, Lila, tu as vraiment tout compris. Bien mieux
que Spinoza.
LILA Miaoo!
BAPHOMET Ouah! Ouah!

_Ils s'enlacent, s'embrassent. Ils sont éclairés par un réflecteur
concentrique. Baphomet lève les yeux et, clignant de l'œil, sournois, au
public, sourit embarrassé. Puis il appuis sur un bouton et recommence
à l'embrasser. Sur eux tombe un petit rideau avec écrit : NOIR. La
scène est envahie par des monstres de tout type et dimensions._

UN MONSTRE La comédie est finie.
AU AUTRE MONSTRE E finita la commedia.
UN EXORCISTE La paix soit avec vous!
TOUS Amen!

Noir.

www.ingramcontent.com/pod-product-compliance
Lightning Source LLC
LaVergne TN
LVHW042152190726
843493LV00006B/1624